HUMOR IN PARADISE

A Jovial Jaunt to Jerk your Junk

By

DEONARAINE RAMDEO

DISCLAIMER

The characters, content, and context have no bearing or resemblance to real persons or circumstances, alive or dead. All names of people and places mentioned in this book are fictitious and imaginary. Any coincidence or reference within the Bahamian setting and structure are an illusion. All jokes are fiction, not facts. The intention is to humor, not to humiliate. No judgment or criticism is intended. Enjoy with an open mind.

UNITED STATES
Lake Okeechobee
Little Bahama Bank
LITTLE ABACO ISLAND
GRAND BAHAMA I.
ABACO ISLAND
ATLANTIC OCEAN
26°
BIMINI ISLANDS
BERRY ISLANDS
NEW PROVIDENCE ISLAND
ELEUTHERA
Straits of Florida
GREAT
Cay Sal Bank (BAHAMAS)
ANDROS ISLAND
THE BAHAMAS
Exuma Sound
CAT ISLAND
SAN SALVADOR ISLAND
RUM CAY
24°
BAHAMA
ANGUILLA CAYS (BAHAMAS)
GREAT EXUMA ISLAND
LONG ISLAND
SAMANA CAY
Tropic of Cancer
CROOKED ISLAND
ACKLINS I.
MAYAGUANA ISLAND
BANK
LONG CAY
RAGGED ISLAND
Caicos Passage
22°
TURKS AND CAICOS ISLANDS (U.K.)
C U B A
Gulf of Ana Maria
Cauto
GREAT INAGUA ISLAND
INAGUA NATIONAL PARK
20°
CARIBBEAN SEA
HAITI
DOMINICAN REPUBLIC
JAMAICA
18°
0   100   200 mi
0   150   300 km
© 2008 Encyclopædia Britannica, Inc.

INTRODUCTION

"Humor in Paradise" is a short novel that captures fun, facts, and features of the beautiful Bahamas. It is a deliberate attempt to present a capsule of the country to the reading public, especially potential visitors to the Bahamas. Basically, it promotes and advertises the small nation on the world stage through literal humor. The major part of the book encompasses one hundred and fifty jokes captured in contexts and settings that are truly Bahamian. These jokes are by no means original; They represent a product of humorous content extracted from literature, conversations, and dramatic episodes. The author owes a debt of gratitude to the original sources of these jokes. The countless authors' original works are acknowledged and appreciated. At the end of each joke, a **MORAL** is included as a delightful lesson for inspiration and knowledge.

The poems in the book are the author's original creative works. They focus on facts and features that highlight the Bahamas. Readers, especially visitors and tourists to the Bahamas, will glean a glamorous guide to this paradise.

ACKNOWLEDGEMENT

The author hereby acknowledges the contributions of the original joke authors, whose jokes were captured and recycled in a different context in the novel. The book serves as a transmitter of joyful content to posterity and a source of pleasure for the reading public.

No personal claim or assumption is made by the author about the originality and sources of the jokes.

DEDICATION

This novel is dedicated to my loving wife, Bibi, who has been a significant supporter of the production of "Humor in Paradise. It is also dedicated to my son, Pooran Ramdeo, and family.

It is also dedicated to all the countless Bahamians whom I have met and known over my four decades of life and work in the six islands of the beautiful Bahamas. This is my humble legacy and contribution to a country that I have grown to love and appreciate.

BIRTH OF THE BAHAMAS

Cannot be said with certainty
How the Bahamas came to be.
Whether it all began
As a result of the Big Bang,
Or it's a prime, proud product
Of the Creator's wonderful handiwork.
Born of the belly of the earth,
Cast and crafted from limestone dirt,
Pristine peaks perched on oceanic mountains,
Floating on the crest of the Atlantic fountain,
Cascading into the Caribbean Sea,
Covered in glorious greenery.
Scattered in turquoise waters,
700 islands are lonely, without human encounters.
Sitting solidly in a steady stream,
Basking and beckoning to the sunbeam,
Whispering to the wild waves,
Slamming steadily on bays and caves.
Shaping shores and building beaches
With smooth or ragged, rugged outreaches,
Innocently, patiently poised
Like a lass with no cosmetic disguise,
Anxiously waiting for an earnest
Embrace from the hands of the human race.

These pristine, idyllic islands
Were first inhabited by the Lucayans,
Who fled fear from another territory,
Defying the limits of geography
Depending on Nature to survive.
They stayed for centuries till Columbus arrived.
Opening the way for Europeans,
Who eventually sealed the fate of the Lucayans.
Later, Adventurers arrived in Eleuthera,
Sailing all the way from Bermuda.
Then came the Loyalists from the USA,
Bringing their slaves here to stay.
Establishing plantations required manual labor,
So they brought enslaved people from Africa.
Thus, Bahamian society changed a lot
As the population became a melting pot.
Over the years, being a crown colony,
Evolving from proprietorship and slavery,
And a political structure of white dominance,
Till Majority Rule ushered in independence.
Predominantly black in population today,
The Bahamas is making great headway,
Together proudly marching forward
And boldly going upward and onward.

THE BEAUTIFUL BAHAMAS

The Bahamas is an archipelagic nation,
700 islands scattered in the Atlantic Ocean,
Located in a sub-tropical geographical arena
Between the capitalist USA and the communist Cuba,
70 miles via sailing encounter,
Less than an hour flight from Florida.
Richly blessed by bewitching beauty
Of abundant sun, sand, and sea,
Natural resources of enviable attraction
To visitors from every global nation.
A small nation with less than a million people,
Courteous, friendly, and very hospitable,
A proud product of chequered, rich history
That preceded the days of discovery
Made by Christopher Columbus in 1492,
Disturbing the peace of the indigenous crew.
Spanish influence and establishment did surrender
To the ownership of British Lord Proprietors.
Later, the British Monarchs showed intensified interest,
Conquering, colonizing the Bahamas to invest
In the development of productive colonies,
Reaping profits to swell the British treasuries,
Suppressing piracy and establishing a vibrant plantocracy
That introduced the sufferance of slavery,
Bringing thousands of people from African nations
To provide long-suffering labor to plantations.

British occupation and colonization lasted for centuries
Until the day of Independence in July 1973.
Today, about 30 islands have inhabitants and residents,
But the bulk of the population live in New Providence.
Nassau in New Providence is the capital city,
Having the seat of government to run the country.
Being a democratic Monarchy,
The British King is the symbolic Head of the country.
Tourism plays a dominant role in the economy,
While banking and commerce play second fiddle.
The Bahamas is a developing country with a fairly healthy GDP.
The Bahamian dollar is at par with the US dollar;
Both are used interchangeable at every counter.
Cost of living is by no means cheap;
Surviving entails going in the pocket very deep.
Like other countries in the international sphere,
Socio-economic classes exist here.
Rich and the privileged sit at the top of the hierarchy,
While the poor occupy the lowest rung in society,
And the middle class stay in between
As buffer connecting the two extremes.
Based on a comprehensive Constitution,
The Bahamas is a law-abiding, Christian nation.
Crime level is low but variable;
Folks need to be cautious, mindful, and responsible.
In The Bahamas, freedom and beauty shine,
Where people freely play and have a good time.
Bahamas cuisine in a bowl or plate,

Tempted and tasty to the palate.
The variety of local dishes and seafood
Leave one satisfied and feeling good.
Climate is mostly on the sunny side,
With an average Fahrenheit temperature of 75.
Cool and pleasant during winter months,
Warm and welcome in summer months.
There's a variety of accommodation in which to dwell,
Ranging from Airbnb to luxury hotel,
Costly during peak seasons;
Early reservation is of good reason.
Millions of visitors come to The Bahamas annually
To have fun in its sun, sand, and sea,
Soaking skins in crystal clear turquoise water,
Fishing, sailing, jetskiing at leisure,
Sunbathing on stretches of sandy shores,
Getting the desired tan lying on white beaches galore.
Tourists gravitate to the local places of attraction
Scattered on the spread of exotic islands.
The amazing Atlantis found on Paradise Island,
One of two found on the global strand.
Old forts bedecked with ancient cannons,
Reminiscent of the vital need for protection.
The Queen's Stairway takes folks up a hill
That captures scenic sights your eyes to fill.
Specimen of the flourish of flora and fauna
Displayed at the Adastra Gardens in Nassau.
A visit to the stupendous Straw market

Reveals the native skills, creativity, and wit.
An evening out to the famous Fish fry
Will leave one happy and high.
Bahamas' natural beauty, charm, and aura
Make it a true, tourist Mecca.

LAUGHTER

"Tis a good and rewarding thing
To make laughter your miracle machine,
Producing joy and longevity
To your life on this earthly journey.

Laughter is the best remedy
To troubles and tragedy.
Comedy creates a road to relief
To sadness and grief.

Hearty, liberal laugh
Makes muscles unwind, taking a day off.
Nerves relax and rejoice in this,
And the brain benefits from a breadth of bliss.

He who laughs in the face of failure
Surely is a soul superior.
He who falls flat in the face of failure
Can recover with a fit of laughter.

Never laugh at someone's shortcomings or suffering.
Join in the celebration of their success
And sense the joy of climbs and crests.

When someone criticizes you,
Don't get mad or blue.
Defeat it with a chuckle
And watch your critic cringe and crumble.

He who has no sense of humor
Misses the mirth and melody life has to offer.
Fish for fun, crack jokes,
Flocking with funny, friendly folks.

Never take life seriously,
Prostrating to the pressure of every day's responsibility.
Take time out of your busy schedule,
Seeking solace in refreshing ridicule.

When cornered by complication or confusion,
Just smile in profusion,
Waiting for the dark clouds to clear,
Giving the leverage and latitude to change gear.

When disappointments drive you down under,
Don't flounder on the floor and surrender.
Review circumstances as a comedy of errors
By resorting to lifts of laughter.

Laughter unlocks the fullness of life
Without the rigors of stress and strife.
Let laughter be your sunshine,
Providing light, radiant and sublime.

Greet each new day with a smile or laugh,
Sweetening the spirit to set you off,
Lightening, lifting your mind and heart,
Affording a splendid spark and a cheerful start.

Learn to laugh lively with vigor
At or with the person in the mirror,
Accepting and loving yourself for what you are,
Elevating the ego to reach the star.

Laugh freely to get high and happy;
This will surely shut down the pharmacy.
Find someone, something to make you laugh,
Or make someone laugh his/her head off.

JOKES

Nassau-NY Nicety

A Bahamian became friends with a NY tourist who invited him to visit USA. Whilst sight-seeing in NY the Bahamian asked " How long did they take to build the twin towers? "

With concrete confidence the Yankee said: "Two weeks ".

Passing by the Empire State Building he asked "How long did they take to build that? '

In a bold breadth the Yankee answered: "One week".

During a return visit to the Bahamas the Bahamian picked up the Yankee at the airport and whilst passing the Mega Bahamar Complex the Yankee remarked: "Wow! What a fantastic collection of huge hotels.

How long did they take to build such a monster?

"Bahamian: " Last night when I passed here that wasn't there."

MORAL: A witty lie can save your day. Lies are more creative, colorful and captivating than truth.

Demented Dimension

Conversation between two elderly men

Sidney: "Hi! What you looking for?"

James: " My boat. I don't remember where I moored it."

Sidney: " I know that feeling."

James: "What! You can't find your boat too?"

Sidney: "Really I'm trying to figure out if I came here by boat or I

flew in.

MORAL: When your memory playing games take along your grandson.

Geographical Gimmick

In a Social Studies class, the teacher displayed a map of the Caribbean and asked: "Andrew, come and find the Bahamas on this map. " Andrew correctly pointed it out. Teacher then asked: " Now class tell me who discovered the Bahamas."

The class shouted; " Andrew did. "

MORAL: When one fails to make specific correlation with issues at hand shocking surprises emerge.

The Precious Prize

A man had half a bottle rum in his back pocket and whilst he was disembarking Bahamas Air he fell down from the plane's step. Flat on the ground he felt liquid oozing from his body. In high hopes he remarked: "Oh God, let it be blood."

MORAL: Get your priority right even if you are on the wrong lane. People place premium on things that they value even if they are insignificant to others.

Sounds from the Sky

A 6-year-old Exumian couldn't stand his 3-year-old brother loud, endless crying. So, he asked his mom; " Mummy where did he come from?

" Mom: " From Bahamas air flying in the sky. "

6-year-old: " Aha! No wonder the stewardess threw him out."

MORAL: A sweet lie produces a sour response.

The Rude Reprisal

Teacher: "Jim, how old are you?" Jim put up 4 fingers.

Teacher: " How many books do you have in your bag?" Jim put up 2 fingers.

Teacher: "Can't you talk?"

Jim: " Can't you count? "

MORAL: Never underestimate the wisdom of children.

Fast Fathers

Three boys were trading lies. First one said: " My dad is so fast he can run a mile before your spit reaches the ground."

Second one said:" My dad can shoot at a target and he gets therebefore the bullet does."

Third boy said: "Piece ah cake! My dad works at Ministry of Works. He knocks off at 5 pm. He's so fast he reaches home by 3 pm. "

MORAL: You save a lot when you work for government.

Delayed Death

Two condemned prisoners were offered their last fabulous meals. The first one requested ham, turkey, chicken, peas-n-rice and guava- duff which he promptly got.

The second one asked for pineapples and guineps. The executioner said: "We have none of that. They are out of season right now."

Condemned man said: " No problem, man! I'll wait."

MORAL: Quick thinking can delay death.

The Bountiful Burial

A guy, whose favorite pet died, went to an established church in Nassau and asked the priest-in-charge if he could give his dog a decent funeral. The priest gazed at him with spiritual surprise." What!! We don't do animal funeral. But I suggest that you go over the hill and ask one of those jumper churches to do it. I'm sure they will."

The guy slowly walked away and the priest smiled that he got rid of him. But the guy turned around and asked: " Father if I give them $5000 you think they'll do it?" Instantly the priest gasped:" Why you didn't tell me the dog was Catholic!"

MORAL: Everything has a price in this world. Please don't take religion to the dogs.

The Beautiful Boomerang

A father noticed his grown son wasting his life away, unemployed and always asking for hand-outs. So, he decided to have a talk with him.

He said:" Son when Hon. Hubert Ingraham was your age he was working in the day and studying in the night to be a lawyer. Look at you! You are good for nothing."

The son gave his father a long look then said:" Dad, when Mr. Ingraham was your age, he was the Prime Minister of the Bahamas."

MORAL: Getting a taste of your own medicine is bitter. Think before you talk.

Good Guidance

A guidance officer at a popular high school in New Providence was asked by the principal to deliver the fatal news to a student, Danny Rolle, whose mother has suddenly died. Armed with his special skills in psychology the guidance officer went to the class where Danny was. He said:" All those who have mothers leave the class and proceed to the corridor."

Everyone went outside. As Danny was going out of the door the officer shouted:

"Danny, where the hell you think you're going? Stay right yah!"

MORAL: There are many ways to skin a cat.

Ugly Urgency

Five friends flew out from Inagua to Nassau and went to get a taxi to go downtown.

Wanting to go together they all rushed into a taxi on duty. The driver made the comment: " Legally I can only carry four passengers and myself, a total of five, now we have six, so one must come out. Here is the deal..... the ugliest must come out"

One of the five friends said: "When you come out, who will drive? "

MORAL: Your advice can rebound and hurt you.

13

Sweet Salvation

An armed robber invaded a woman's house in a remote village in Abaco and with pointed gun demanded of her.

"Life, money or sex!"

Courageously the woman said:" I have no money, and I don't want to die."

MORAL: In any difficult situation there is always a way out.

Senile Sensibility

The same robber went to rob a man. He demanded:" Common man, money or life?"

Cornered the man said:" I am keeping my money for old age."

MORAL: Love of money will destroy all of us.

Something Sane

At our asylum in Sandilands a doctor saw an inmate fishing in a bucket of water.

Not wanting to tell the inmate it was useless activity he enquired:" Why are you doing that?"

The nut said:" Doc if you don't do something here, they think you are" crazy.

MORAL: Even insanity has some measure of creativity.

The Heroic Humbug

At the same asylum a psychiatrist noticed a hulk of a guy rescued a drowning man at the pool. Later in the day he went to congratulate the guy for his heroic deed. "That was a brave thing you did to save the drowning man. Tell me, where is he right now? " Indifferent to the doctor's compliment the hulk in a causal manner answered:" He was so wet I hung him up by the neck on my ceiling to dry."

Moral: Not every brave deed can make one a hero.

The Spelling Size

Teacher asked Johnny to spell "cow". Johnny started bravely " Koo.." The class erupted in laughter. He got two cuts for getting it wrong. Hollering in tears he ran to his home nearby to complain. He told his dad the teacher beat him for nothing. Angry dad took Johnny to class with a 2x4 in his hand. He barged in class and demanded to know why the teacher beat his son. After the teacher explained what happened the father said:" Teacher, why you so unfair? Lil Johnny can't spell a big thing like cow. Why you didn't ask him to spell something small like mosquito?

MORAL: Kicking cow produce kicking calf.

The Inverted Interview

Two old buddies went for an interview for a mechanic job at the new Bahamar Complex. The smarter one was called in first and had to answer three questions. Bossman asked: " How old are you? "

Mechanic said: "35"

Bossman: "How many years' experiences do you have?"

Mechanic: "5"

Bossman: "Theoretical and practical?"

Mechanic: "Both" He got the job."

Outside his friend enquired how did the interview go. Quickly he told him that he would be asked three questions and the answers were; -35:5: Both

When he was called the Bossman switched the questions.

Bossman: "How many years' experiences do you have as a mechanic?"

Friend: "35"

Bossman: "Wow! How old are you?"

Friend: "5. This clearly made the Bossman angry."

Bossman: "Damn! You think I'm an ass or a fool!?"

Friend: "Both"

MORAL: Always be prepared for the unexpected.

The Shitty Slide

A boss came in unexpectedly in his second-floor office at the Traffic Dept. in Nassau and caught one of the workers red-highhandedly stealing money from his drawers.

The embarrassed worker ran out of the office and slid down to the first floor hurting himself badly. Later he was recounting the story to a close pal. The pal offered some sympathy by saying:" Boy, if it was me. I would a shit on me skin". To which his friend replied: "What you think I was sliding on? "

MORAL: Stealing reveals your filth.

Insane Insult

A young man had a flat whilst driving pass the Sandilands asylum. He took his spares and jack out and began changing the wheels. Whilst doing it the four lugs accidentally fell in a deep ditch nearby. This upset him and he started to kick the car. From inside the fenced compound of the asylum an inmate was observing everything and he suggested to the young man to take a lug each from the other three wheels and fix on the spares until he got to the mechanic shop. After he did that, he faced the inmate and asked: "What you doing in deh?"

Inmate replied: "What you doing out deh? "

MORAL: Insanity has its sparks of genius. There are more lunatics outside the asylum.

The Gender Gimcrack

A half-drunk man mistakenly went into the ladies restroom at Fish fry in Arawak Cay in Bay Street. After relieving himself and was walking out a woman was going in. Surprised to see the man in the ladies' restroom she remarked: "This is for ladies!" in a stern voice. In defense the man put his hand over his crotch and said: "And so is this!"

MORAL: Let sleeping dogs lie. No public rebuke in a private setting

Defying the Doctor

A middle-aged woman from Ragged Island went to visit Dr. Nottage. Whilst doing the check-up the good doctor initiated a conversation. "For a 50 yrs. woman you are in top shape."

Woman: "Who says I'm 50? I'm 65 yrs. Old."

Doctor: "Holy Smoke! Then your mom must have lived to a ripe old age."

Woman: "Who says my mom is dead? She will be 85 next week."

Doctor: "Holy Cow! Then your grammaa must have lived long too."

Woman: "Who says my grammy dead? She will be 105 next month and she's getting married on the 25th."

Doctor: "Holy Shit!! Why would an old woman like that want to get married.

Woman: "Who says she wants to get married?" The good doc closed clinic and went home to think about ways to live long.

MORAL: Don't judge a book by its cover. When you dig deep you discover wealth.

The Spanish Sequence

Two passengers, sitting near each other, on a plane started to talk. One was a Spanish teacher. He asked the other where he was going. "I' m going to Rio Janiero and then to San Juan" with heavy emphasis on the "J". In a polite way the teacher told him that " J " is silent in the Spanish language and proceeded to ask, "When will you return?"

"If not --anuary maybe in --une or --uly. " His " Js" were very silent.

MORAL: Careful how you teach new tricks to old dogs.

Theological Titles

Three boys were under a tree in Cat Island boasting about their uncles.

First said: "My uncle is a priest at St. Matthews. When people see him on the road they say 'Reverend Father'."

Second said:" My uncle is the Bishop at Christ the King. When people see him, they say ' Your Highness '

Third said:" That aren't nothing! My uncle is 7 feet tall and he weighs 600 pounds. When he walks down the road people say 'Oh my God '

MORAL: When wits of reverence meet holy sparks fly out.

Appetizing Appeal

A rich farmer in Andros took his friends on a tour of his huge farm boasting about the variety and quantity of crops he was cultivating.

About half of a mile into his field they saw a guy quickly picking ripe fruits and loading them in a bag. The farmer knew that this stranger was stealing his fruits but he didn't want to embarrass him in his friends' presence. The thief tried to be nice by greeting the farmer.

Thief: "Good morning Mr. Russell. You are out early."

Farmer Russell: "Oh yes. We're getting appetite for our breakfast. What are you up to?"

Thief: "I am getting breakfast for my appetite."

MORAL: Tit for tat is fair play, especially when hunger strikes

The Loud Landing

A young man took his blind friend to steal coconuts in West end Grand Bahama. He climbed the tree and started to kick down coconuts. Accidentally he fell from the tree and landed with a loud thump on the ground. When his blind friend heard the sound he remarked, "One more like that and we're good to go!"

MORAL: What you don't see won't hurt you

27

The Grammar Grade

In the one-room schoolhouse in Mayaguana Mr. Williams was giving a student a warning. "Peter, you keep saying and writing poor grammar.........I has.... we does_you is...... If you keep doing that your grade in English will not improve."

Peter: "Sir, I do lissen to you with both ears but everything gone out the other ear."

Mr. Williams: "Wait, how come you get three ears now?"

Peter; "Muddah sick! I even bad at math's."

MORAL: Sometimes the best game is to lose.

28

Incurable Injustice

A fellow was walking along Sugar Beach on Berry Island and he found a bottle on the shore. He unscrewed the cork and out came a genie.

Genie thanked him for the release and asked him to name two wishes one of which he would grant.

Fellow: " Build me a bridge from Berry Island to Nassau. I can't travel by boat cause I get sea-sick and I am scared of flying"

Genie: "That's an impossible task. What's your second wish?"

Fellow: "Teach me how to get rid of these corrupt politicians who make big promises they don't keep."

Genie: "How you want the bridge, two lanes or four lanes?"

MORAL: There is no cure for corruption in politics

Parental Practice

A six-year-old was asked by her teacher to spell the word "neat"

Child: "Neat."

Teacher: Correct. What does it mean?

Child: "Without soda or ice."

Teacher: "Spell the word 'straight'"

Child: "S-t-r-a-i-g-h-t"

Teacher: "Correct again. What does it mean?"

Child: "Without ice"

Teacher then asked the child to use both words in one sentence

Child: "My dad drinks neat and my mom swallows straight."

MORAL: Children pay close attention to drunken parents.

Exclusive Excitement

In a one room schoolhouse in Rum Cay a teacher asked class to draw something exciting on a blank page.

Students jumped at the opportunity to show off their creative skills.

Each pupil had to go in front of the class to display and explain his or her art piece. The first showed a zizzag on his page and said it was the lightening The next went out and proudly exposed a funnel like shape.

"What is that, Mark?" Asked the teacher.

"That's a tornado. It can be scary as well as fascinating to look at." said Mark.

"And Johnny what is that?" Enquired the teacher Spell out what Johnny did. He put a period. dot.

"Miss, in grammar this is a period which is placed at the end of a sentence. Last summer when my 15-year-old sister missed hers for a month there was commotion in our house."

MORAL: A dot of imagination can create a cascade of creativity.

The Easy Essay

Another class was asked to write a descriptive essay on a baseball match they witnessed. Every student got busy putting their thoughts down on paper. Teacher noticed smart Alec at the back smiling with abandon relief and asked: "Alec are you finished?"

"Yes Miss." Teacher looked at his paper and saw only a series of dots and asked him to explain. Alec: "Miss these are drops representing rain. No play because of rain." Alec failed but he received compliments for his novel idea.

MORAL: Not all short-cuts are beneficial.

The Savior Saves

In L N Coakley's high in Exuma school students were asked a hypothetical question in computer class. "Jesus and the Devil were doing power-point test. Just as they finished blackout came on. When the electricity was restored who you think won?"

Vanessa answered: "Neither of them because they would have lost their data"

Julian responded: "Jesus wins because Jesus saves."

MORAL: Faith in the Lord can bring light to your life

Modern Miracle

In C R Walker High students were asked to describe how Jesus healed the lame man. One student, whose parents always bought him the latest high-tech gadgets, wrote the following: When a close friend saw the lame man groaning on the floor he quickly googled to find out where Jesus was.

Then he called Jesus on his cell phone and asked Him to help out. Inside 5 minutes an impressive car pulled up at the lame man's residence. Jesus hurriedly came out of the limousine and rushed to the spot where the sick man lay. He miraculously picked him up and threw him in the back seat and sped off to Doctors' Hospital where the man was healed.

The friend later texted Jesus a sincere note of gratitude. Jesus tweeted" No problem"

MORAL: Technology can be a great tool if put to good use. But don't worship it as God.

The Dicey Dude

Two boys became friends in a New Providence neighborhood. One is a born city boy and the other is from Ragged Island. In a conversation one day the city boy said: "My dad is a great fisherman. He recently caught a fish 3 feet in length."

The boy from Ragged retorted: "Hush you mouth! My dad back home uses sizes like that as baits."

MORAL: Bigger can be better if you lace it with lies.

The Naming Narrative

During the eighties in the Bahamas lots of money came in from drug dealings.

One husband stored about a million dollars and proudly said to the wife: "Sweetie, we'll store this up for hard times. You know Mr. Hardtime always come. Go hide this until hard time comes." Dutifully the wife securely concealed the bag of cash.

Outside was a guy listening to husband and wife talk through an opened window.

He waited until the husband left the house to go on another deal. Then he came to the door and knocked. The wife opened the door and saw this fresh face.

In a matter-of-fact manner he said: "Good morning, ma'am, My name is Mr. Hardtime and I have come to pick up my package." Remembering what her husband told her she quickly brought the bag of money and gave it to Mr. Hardtime.

Later that night when her husband returned, she smiled and said:" Mr. Hardtime came by for his money which I gave to him." The husband hit the roof: " Stupid woman! Why you did such a dumb thing!!"

"Ain't you tell me…. you telling me the money was for 'Hardtime'?"

MORAL: Unspecific instructions can bring your downfall.

The Spelling Spectacle

A new recruit in the police force apprehended a traffic violator in Charlotte St. He started to write out the charge sheet but could not spell Charlotte so he took the man to Bay Street to complete writing out the charge. He could spell Bay.

MORAL: Use your feet when your head fails you.

Prestine Prize

Teen at a prom in Nassau was recounting an experience he had at Science Show in New York. He saw a number of replicas of police men brains on sale. Among them was the brain of a Caribbean policeman. He noticed that it was the most expensive one. Curious he wanted to know why, so he enquired.

"Excuse me Sir, can you tell me why the Caribbean policeman's brain is so expensive?"

The seller quickly responded: "That brain was never used!"

MORAL: Brand new things are priceless compared to second-hands.

The height of Honesty

A very honest young man passed by a Chinese restaurant in Collins Avenue and was taken back by the delicious aroma emanating from the eatery. He had no money so he prayed that he got a **$20.** to enjoy a tasty meal. Saddened he walked on and lo be hold he saw three $20s on the ground. Slowly he picked up only one and proceeded to have his desired meal.

MORAL: Taking just what you need is the art of contentment

Divine Discrimination

There is racialism all over the world and even in heaven. Three Bahamians died and went straight to heaven's gate where St. Peter questioned them before getting entry. The white Bahamian was called first and was asked: "How many ships did Columbus and his crew use on his first voyage?"

White man: "Three." St. Peter directed him to the gate of heaven. Secondly, he summoned the brown Bahamian and asked him "How many sailors were on the three ships?"

"200." correctly answered the brown man. He was sent to through the Pearly Gate.

Last it was the black Bahamian's turn. With a serious face St. Peter regarded him.

"I want you to name all those 200 men." Dispirited the black man bent his head and walked towards the gate of Hell.

MORAL: Racialism is a universal curse that won't go away soon.

The Female Force

A psychiatrist in Freeport was conducting a survey of 100 men to find out what percentage of them are hen-pecked and what percentage are their own boss. He created two lines which he named hen-pecked and he-men. Then he announced to the gathering of men and their wives. "I want you men to be very honest. If you listen to and take orders from your wives (hen-pecked) please go in the hen-pecked line. If you think you are a he-man please go in the he-men line.

99% shyly join the hen-pecked line and only one went in the he-men line. The good doctor was surprised at his findings. He praised the lone man for being his own boss and man of the house. Then he asked him:" Who told you to go in that line?"

"My wife", replied the man.

MORAL: Modern women have become bosses of their homes and are proud to wear the pants.

Grotesque Gossip

Every year an established Church in the Bahamas holds a retreat for its priests where they unwind, recoup and strategize. In the year that it was held in Eleuthera. Three priests teamed up in solitude after a long session. One suggested that they bared their chests to release stress: "We all have moral failings. It will be good to confess. I will start. I ' m sweet hearting two beautiful women in my church." To which the second one added: "I have a weakness for gambling. I usually take money from the collection plate and sneak in at Island Luck to play." The third man of the cloth was very shy and reluctant to make his confession. Encouraged by the other two he sheepishly said: "I am a terrible gossip."

MORAL: Keep your skeleton in the cupboard.

Makeshift Madness

A farmer was passing by the Sand I lands asylum with a truck load of cow shit (manure) and one of the inmates asked: "What you're gonna do with that? " The patient farmer said:" I'm going to put it on my tomatoes."

To which the inmate responded: "We put Ranch dressing on our tomatoes and people say we are crazy."

MORAL: There is a thin line between sanity and madness.

Double Dose

A BEC worker approached Mr. Francis, the pay clerk and started to row. "What's going down man! You deducted 2 hours of my overtime pay. Why?" Mr. Francis: "Last month when we overpaid you by 2 hours you didn't row." Worker: Look here homeboy I can deal with one mistake but not two. Pay up!"

MORAL: Mistakes can be costly to some and beneficial to others.

The Exasperating Exchange

Two accountants exchanged words whilst going up the elevator to their office at Atlantis on Paradise Island. One said: "Yesterday I got a rabbit for my whining son."

Other accountant: "Good trade."

MORAL: Accountants don't know the value of human beings.

Contaminated Confession

A drunk entered a church in Nassau and went straight to the confession booth. The priest heard him settling down and waited for the sinful utterance. After what seemed like a long silence the priest rapped a couple of times to get his attention. Finally, the drunk said: "There's no toilet paper here too"

MORAL: Blessed are the drunks for they shall get relief.

Migratory Misfortune

In a history class Miss. Turnquest started off by saying: "When the New World was opened up Europeans came to the Bahamas in great numbers. Tell me class who were some of these people."

Shakina in a went first: "Some of them who lost their property decided to come here."

Edniqua added: "Some who lost their families in wars came to make a fresh start."

Joshua followed closely in similar opening: "Some of them who lost their lives came looking for a living." The teacher, a believer in reincarnation, gave them full marks.

MORAL: Not all role models are good examples.

Sacred Sinners

During a Sunday sermon the pastor told the congregation in All Saints Church in Crroked Island that next week he would preach about "Thou shall not tell lies" and suggested that they read up Matthew chapter 29.

Before he started his sermon the following Sunday he asked: "How many of you read Matthew 29?" All the hands went up.

Pastor: "Matthew only has 28 chapters. Anyway, now to the sins of telling lies."

MORAL: Lies can never be a cool, convenient Savior.

Communication Closure

A University of the Bahamas first year student returned to San Salvador to spend the spring break holidays with his parents. The mother was so glad to see him so initiated conversation with him: "Jack it's so nice to have you here for the two weeks. Aren't you happy to be back? " Jack just nodded. She tried again;" UB must be interesting. Do you like it there?" Jack barely said "yep". She tried once more to engage him in a conversation:" Tell me about your studies and friends." To which Jack said; "Okay."

Not giving up mother asked; "What is your major?" "Communications" replied Jack.

MORAL: Modern universities know how to shorten courses at a high price.

The Monetized Marriage

After mass at St. Agnes Anglican in Nassau a married man approached the priest and said: "Father you just preached that people shouldn't profit from other people's mistake. Do you strongly believe in that?" "Of course I do!" asserted the good priest.

Married man: "Then you should return the $300 you charged me for marrying me to my wife last year."

MORAL: Some mistakes can be very costly.

Stranded on Sex

A big businessman had to make a speech at a weekly meeting. He was hard pressed with time so he didn't prepare anything worthwhile so he talked about SEX. When he returned home his wife asked him what he spoke on he lied: "Sailing."

The next day as she was shopping at Super value in Mackey Street she bumped into one of her husband's associates, who remarked: "That was a great speech your husband made."

"Oh, he only did it twice. The first time he fell off and the second time he was sea-sick."

MORAL: Lies will destroy your integrity.

The Ideal Idol

A Sunday school teacher in Nichol's Town, Andros asked the class: "Why do you think the Israelites made a Golden Calf?"

Six-year-old Barnabas demanded: "Me Miss! They didn't have enough gold to build a big cow."

MORAL: During the formative years children's brains fire fast.

52

The Reactionary Remedy

"Mummy!" shouted sick little Johnny from his bed. "I'm very sick, please call the Vet."

"A Vet!!" asked mummy. "Why not a doctor?"

"At school I work like a horse, the other kids treat me like a dog and I grunt like a pig, and when I come home, I have to answer to a " gussemae cow."

MORAL: If you think like an animal you behave as one.

53

A Medical Mishap

A patient visited his doctor and complained. "Doc, I have a weak back."

"How long now you're suffering from a weak back? " Enquired the doctor.

"A week back." answered the sick man.

"Now stop playing games!" warned the doctor.

"True, it's a week back." insisted the patient.

MORAL: If you are consistent, you can confuse any genius.

The Flaming Fire

A Five-year-old Denny was absent from school for a week. When here turned the teacher chided him. "Ducking Denny, why have you been absent for so long?"

"Sorry Sir. My dad got burnt." "Lying boy! Nothing serious eh" exclaimed the teacher. "Sir, those guys don't play games at the crematorium."

MORAL: This world would be a better place when teachers exercise more patience and sympathy.

Fasting Fury

A Bay Street hoodlum walked up to a well-dressed, stout woman and begged for some money to buy food. " Maam I haven't eaten anything for four long days." The over-sized woman replied. " I wish I had your will power. "

MORAL: A tit-for-tat is a damning defense.

The Troublesome Tot

Troublesome little Dick of Dandelion's kindergarten said to his mother: "Mom teacher asked me today if I have any other brothers or sisters who would be coming to school." "So, what did she say when you told her you're the only child?" She said, "Thank God!"

MORAL: Rude and boisterous pupils turn off any teacher

The Delivery of Death

Doctor Robins of Princess Margaret hospital called on one of his patients one evening. He said to the cancer patient: "I have good news and bad news"

"Give me the good news first" requested the terminally ill man.

"You have 24 hours to live" lamented the doctor.

"Holy Cow! If that's the good news what can the bad one be?

The doctor held his hand and whispered "I forgot to tell you this yesterday."

MORAL: Hospitals kill more people than a happy home.

A Sexual Second

A berserk woman from over the hill barged in a rich politician's office and carried on bad.

"My daughter works in your house as a servant and you got her pregnant. Why you took advantage of her?"

The politician compromised "If she is pregnant, I'll give you $10, 000"

To which the calmed down woman agreed: "You are so kind. If she is not pregnant, will you give her another chance?"

MORAL: The love of money is the fountain of all evil.

Sleepy Sermon

In the middle of a very long sermon a man walked out of church unceremoniously. At the end of the service the wife of the man walked up to the bishop to explain; "Bishop I know that you felt bad when Henry walked out of your sermon."

"Oh yes, that was discouraging indeed." claimed the bishop.

"Please don't feel bad. You see Henry keeps walking out of his sleep since childhood days."

MORAL: People get drowsy when things get boring. Keep lectures and sermons short and sweet.

Furious Faith

An old woman who had immovable faith in God was asked to leave her home and go to a hurricane shelter during an approaching monster storm. She strongly resisted claiming that her God would save her. And so, she prayed steadfastly. During the early stage of the hurricane two officers of the RBPF came in a jeep to get her. She refused to go. As the storm worsened two members of the RBDF came to get her. Again, she turned them down. When the storm was raging two veterans from BASRA came to get her to no avail.

Finally, she perished and when she ascended into heaven, she put her case to God. "Almighty I placed so much faith in you but you failed to save me. Why?"

God said "I sent help to you three times and you refused."

MORAL: God works in wondrous ways that surpass all understanding.

Sound Sentencing

A boy boasted to his friend: "My uncle knows exactly when he will die, what date what day and what hour."

"Monkey Uncle! How come he knows that?" Demanded the friend.

"The judge who sentenced him told him so."

MORAL: Somebody somehow in your family will make you proud someday.

Ways of Wealthy Women

At a motivational session in Melia Hotel women were citing ways to show how they transformed their husbands.

First woman said: "I made my husband into a highly successful businessman."

"What was he doing before you did such remarkable transformation?" asked the Moderator. "He was a fish vendor at Potter's Cay."

Second woman volunteered "I made my husband a millionaire." "Amazing! What was he before you did such a trick?" Enquired the Moderator.

"He was a billionaire."

MORAL: A woman could make or break any man.

63

Reciprocal Rebuff

A local surgeon was walking through the cemetery at Gladstone Road when he saw the grave digger taking a break from his digging job and drinking liquor from a bottle.

He slammed the man "Hey you! How dare you drink on the job? Get back to work before I report you." The grave digger took one sip and responded wearily: "I expect you to be the last to complain, bearing in mind all your fatal blunders I have to cover up."

MORAL: When you live in glass house don't throw stones.

64

Fishing with Facts and Faith

The priest in the Anglican church in Georgetown, Exuma was preaching about 'Fact and Faith' and he gave an illustration by pointing at Mr. Marshal, his wife and four children who were sitting in the front pew.

"The wife knows that the children are hers. That's a 'Fact'. On the other hand, Mr. Marshall believes they are his children-----That's 'Faith.'

MORAL: Whichever way you look at its children are blessings from God.

65

Providential Politics

During one general election fever in Governor's Harbor a group of folks were discussing the dynamics of politics.

One observed: "These politicians are so crooked, they feed us with lies." Second chipped in: "Looks like that's their professional trademark."

Third philosophized: "No point telling them to go to go to hell. They are there already trying to expand it to accommodate all of us."

MORAL: Never underestimate the chicanery and craftiness of politicians.

Sacred Strokes

A local painter was contracted to paint a Baptist Church in Acklins. He was singing "Gentle Jesus ....m-e-e-k... a-n-d...m-i-l-d" and was painting very slowly.

The priest-in-charge suggested: "Can't you paint a bit faster to finish the job before Sunday service?"

The guy painted faster as he sang the tune: " Paint you bungie... paint your bungie paint you bungie fast. . .. Paint your ass... paint your ass... paint your ass fast.......

Hearing that priest said; "Go back to your old tune before you defile this church."

MORAL: Smarter the boss, wiser the worker.

Stale Service

A patron visited a restaurant in Nassau and ordered: "A fried chicken in stale grease, cold beans, dried-up macaroni served with cold, oily peas-n-rice and sour salad."

The waiter said: "Sorry sir, we don't fill such order."

Exasperated the patron chimed: "How come! That's what you served me yesterday."

MORAL: Don't repeat past mistakes: learn from them.

A Birthing Breach

A prominent Bishop once said in a congregation in Abaco that Jesus was supposed to have been born in the beautiful Bahamas, but God had difficulty finding one wise man worse yet three. And coming all the way from the East by foot was impossible.

MORAL: It is reassuring that God loves the Bahamas from that time.

The Big, Bad Bully

"Who painted my desk red!" roared a lad in school. Everyone was quiet."

"I will tear his hip up whoever did this," he continued aggressively. Then a huge bully appeared and said, "I did it! What you want do?" The lad surveyed the over-powering figure standing over him then said "Oh, I just wanted to know when you will apply the second coat paint."

MORAL: When the power against you is overwhelming just surrender in good faith.

Transference of Treasure

A rich white woman in Eastern Heights District in New Providence told the black Bahamian man she got married to that when she died, he must put all her money in her coffin. The condescending husband agreed. It so happened that she died.

The guy had told a close friend about this agreed plan. As the undertakers of Bethel Funeral Parlor were about to lower her coffin in the grave the husband put a neat box in the coffin. So, she was buried with all her money.

The friend enquired: "Did you really put all her money in the coffin?" "Oh yea. Being a good Christian, I must be faithful."

"Good grief! You mean to say you put millions in cash in her coffin!" The loyal husband smiled: "I wrote her a cheque."

MORAL: Loyalty can be rewarded in many ways.

Freedom to Fart Freely

During a wedding reception in downtown Nassau a man entered a room and walked past a couple sitting on a bench. Unexpectedly he farted in front of the wife.

Husband jumped up and blurted: "How dare you farted before my wife?"

"Why, was it her turn?"

MORAL: The beauty of language lies in its interpretation.

Freedom to Fume and Fret

A Cuban guy was looking for an apartment to rent in Nassau. Whenever he heard the rates, he complained how costly and rundown they were. One prospective landlord said: You keep complaining about high rental. How was renting cost in Cuba before you left to come here?

Cuban: No complain. It was great.

"Bahamian:" And how was housing conditions?"

Cuban: "Superb. Excellent. No complain."

"Why are you complaining about our rent and housing?"

Cuban: "In Cuba you cannot complain. Here you can do so."

MORAL: Freedom gives the latitude to whine and complain.

The Artful Ass

During a busy Junkanoo season a family island dude came to Nassau and had to stay in a crummy studio because every other room was taken. There were no toilet facilities in the studio and so he emptied his bowels in a sock and flung it through the only window in the middle of the night. He applied a circular motion to give the package momentum to fall far from his spot but that only caused the watery stool to mess the studio up.

Next morning he beckoned a maid and offered her $20. to clean it up. The maid had a long look at the shitty marks around the walls and up the ceiling and said:" I'll give you $50 to tell me how you set your hip to create a mess like that."

MORAL: If you look hard enough you can see art and creativity even in spoils and spillage.

74

The Bullied Boss

A proud Nassauian felt he was fully in charge of his household. One day he put it to a test. He boldly confronted his teenage son and asked: "Who is the boss of this house?"

Son: "Of course, it's you daddy." Then he walked up to his 18year old daughter and intimidated her with this question: "Who is the head of this family?"

"Without question Dad you are the boss." Answered the girl. Gathering courage, he faced his big, burly, beautiful wife and asked the same question.

The wife lifted him and hurled him to the ground, stamped on him and bashed him up.

"Alright, okay. Take it easy" groaned the injured husband, "There's no reason to get mad because you don't know the right answer."

MORAL: In the struggle for power and position leadership changes hands often.

Bartering Blows at the Bar

A small built guy walked into a bar in Mackey Street and ordered a drink. Whilst sipping his drink a big dude next to him landed a karate chop on him sprawling him to the floor. Dazed he got up and asked the hulk why he did that, to which the dude answered: "That's karate from Korea." The small guy tried to finish his drink and leave. Again, the beast high-fell the small man to the ground and smiled: "That's judo from Japan."

The diminutive guy left and later returned. He sneaked behind the big guy and hit him cold and senseless to the floor. The barman who was witnessing everything walked up to see what happened. The small guy said to him: "When he finally comes to his senses tell him that was a Crowbar from Cartwright garage."

MORAL: A small axe can cut down big trees.

The Liquored Lesson

Whenever there was a festive celebration like Christmas a loving father usually gave his young son a shot of liquor saying: "Here son, drink this. It's good for the worms in your system."

When the son became a man, he indulged heavily in hard, consistent drinking and was slowly going down the drains. Becoming aware of this dangerous habit of his son he intervened and asked: "Son, why are you drinking so much?"

"Dad, remember when I was small you used to give me a shot to keep my worms under control. Guess what, those worms have grown to become snakes."

MORAL: When you allow small deeds of indiscretion to fester, they ultimately develop into huge acts of destruction.

The Beauty of Blessed Booze

A pastor in Long Island was preaching about the danger of drinking alcohol. He tried to demonstrate this by filling one glass with gin and one with pure water. He proceeded to put a live worm in each and asked the congregation to observe carefully. After some time, the worm in the gin wriggled to its death and the other worm in the water was swimming around happily. Then the dutiful pastor asked: "What lesson can you learn from that?"

An old woman in the back in a raised voice said: "When you get worms drink gin."

MORAL: Different perspectives or philosophies of life adds spice to living.

Tit for a Tat

In our parliament along the corridors of time there was a violent feud and fury between an opposition female politician and the sitting Prime Minister. Constantly they traded blows and accusations.

During one session matters mounted to the mountain and the female parliamentarian said to the PM: "If you were my husband, I'd poison your whiskey." To which the humble PM replied: "If you were my wife, I'd gladly drink it."

MORAL: " Evil plans can boomerang and destroy the planners.

Pure Puzzles

Towards the end of a lesson in a junior grade in MGM Major High School a teacher, who concluded his lesson prematurely, allowed students to indulge in a puzzle session. One girl offered "What gets wetter the more it dries?"

Smart Alec blurted " Towel! "Then a boy quizzed" Why is six afraid of seven? "Nobody seemed to have a correct or logical answer, so the quizzer calmly said " Because seven ate (eight) nine."

MORAL: Quizzes not only test mental agility but they open crocks and crevices of creativity.

A Way with Words

In a crowded church in Arthur's Town, Cat Island, the pastor was preaching on the incident involving Jonah and his refusal to obey God's command. He said "Jonah tried to duck the dictate of God by sailing away into hiding. Weather got wild and Jonah fell overboard and swallowed a whale...."

Before he could continue a brave boy bellowed "Father, you get it wrong. Jonah didn't swallow the whale. The whale swallowed Jonah."

'Some kind of swallowing happened' replied the Rector rather rashly.

MORAL: Reversing realities can have repulsive repercussion.

81

Climate Crisis

A slick guy from Crooked Island encountered an Australian visitor at Woodes Rodgers walkway in downtown Nassau. They decided to have a beer and watch the cruise ships moored up at Prince George wharf. In the conversation that entailed the Australian said, "Back home we raise pumpkins and sweet potatoes that are extremely huge. They are so gigantic that only one can fit in a dump truck."

"Muddo sick! How' s that possible?" the awed Bahamian said.

"The climate man" voiced the visitor. Not to be outdone the Islander responded, "In Crooked Island we build houses in the air with no steps nor stairways." "So how for the love of Christ do they get in to their houses?" interrupted the tourist. Bahamian proudly proclaimed, "They climate, man."

MORAL: Deception digs up more humor than honesty.

Shitty Seniors

Three elderly men at Ridgeland Park were talking about their early morning movements. The 70-year-old started, "I get up at 8 am and go to the bathroom to do No. 1 and No.2."

The 80-year-old pitched in, "I arise at 7 am and do the same before having breakfast."

The 90-year-old smiled and shrugged "I do No.1 and No.2 earlier than that." Then in one voice the other two seniors asked, "So what time do you get up from bed?"

"I don't get up."

MORAL: Everyone is entitled to the comfort of their beds.

Maternal Mischief

Two female teachers met up at Marathon Mall. Happy to see one another after many years they indulged in a conversation. One enquired of the other, "How are your two sons doing?"

"Oh, fine. The elder one being smart he graduated as a medical doctor."

"And how about the younger one who was not smart and very sly?"

"Oh, him. He became a lawyer."

MORAL: Mothers masterfully move into defense when you be little their offsprings.

Anal Anguish

Farmer Farquason noticed that the fruits in his orchard have been disappearing mysteriously. So, he decided to lay wait in hiding to nab the culprits responsible for such loss. After about two hours he heard noises near his back fence as three teenagers jumped into the farm.

He waited until they completed their illegal acts. As they were about to leave with their loot the farmer suddenly confronted them with a rifle pointed directly at them. He ordered them to stand in a line and empty their bags. When the first on emptied stolen grapes from his bag the farmer ordered him to push them up his anus. The second one had to do the same with the guavas he pilfered. Then they looked at the third guy and began to laugh.

Why you're giggling?" demanded Mr. Farquah son.

Simultaneously the two youngsters said, "He got watermelons in his bag."

MORAL: Knowledge of the dire consequences of illegal acts can reduce the rate of crime considerably.

The Math Magic

A busy mother in Duncan Town, Ragged Island put out five cookies in a platter and asked her two sons to share them.

The elder quickly grabbed three and left two for his brother. The younger brother was embittered and he complained coldly, "You're so mean and greedy to grab three cookies."

The elder brother counteracted, "What would you do if you were asked to share them?"

"I would have shown compassion and take two and give you three."

"Big deal!! In that case you still end up with two so stop whining."

MORAL: There is no compassion in sharing the spoils.

The Golden Mean

A couple of guys assembled at Potter's Cay were discussing the virtues of moderation and taking the middle path in life. One said, "Going to extremes in anything can be dangerous if not deadly, so, it is better to follow the golden mean and take the middle road."

Another one chirped in, "Homeboy when you stay in the middle of the road you get run over. You have to hit the pavement."

MORAL: Moderation is the mother of mediocrity but extreme measures and risks can bring a windfall.

87

Tricks of a Trade

At a party held in the village in Bullock's Harbor Berry Island a man, who obviously had too much to drink, flipped flopped and landed on the hand of a woman who was sitting on a bench. In sharp pain the woman erupted in an emotional burst. "You miserable, good-for- nothing drunkard. You hurt my hand." And she went on discharging a slew of expletives at the end of which the shaken man retorted, "Lady, tomorrow I will be sober but you will remain ugly."

MORAL: Forgiveness fosters more satisfaction and reward than revenge and retaliation.

88

The Treasury of Trust

In South Long Island a young man approached his dad, an owner of an established enterprise, and asked him for advice to set up his own business. Smiling satisfactorily the dad said, Son in business as in anything else you don't trust anyone." He went on to demonstrate his point by asking his son to climb up a tree in their yard.

The boy did as he was told and reached the top of the tree. Then the father said, "OK. Jump to me I'll catch you." The obedient son jumped and the father quickly stepped aside letting the boy fall flat on his belly. In great pain he slowly limped up and addressed his father, " Dad, I trusted you to catch me."

The pa replied, "I told you not to trust anyone."

MORAL: When you trust relatives in business, they take advantage and bring you down.

A Righteous Request

A youth from Moore's' Islands was prompted by wishful thinking to write a letter to God asking for a handout. The letter was addressed as follows:

Most High God,

Father in Heaven

Up above in the Sky

Workers at the local post office saw the letter and were curious to know about the contents. They opened and read it.

The boy had asked God for $100. Knowing that the letter would not reach God to fulfill such request they came together and raised $75. which they sent to the boy on a return mail.

After he found out what was in the letter, he quickly wrote a thank - you note to God.

"Thank you, dear God, for the cash. Next time please send money to me through Western Union and not by mail. The workers at the post office are dishonest and corrupt. They opened my letter and stole $25from the $100 I asked for."

MORAL: Sometimes when you do good you end up holding wood

The Woeful Wish

Three best friends were having a grand time together on a beach in Spanish Wells, Eleuthera. Whilst walking along the beach they came upon a strange looking bottle which they opened. Out came a genie. The grateful genie decided to reward them with a wish each. The first one asked for a luxurious home equipped with everything in NY. Granted. The second wished for a mansion in Dubai. Granted.

The last guy felt lonely because he missed his two friends, so he said, "I missed my buddies, please return them to me." Granted.

MORAL: Loneliness is the enemy to happiness and prosperity.

A Purile Passionate Plea

A very smart, gifted lad in Rock Sound, Eleuthera had a conversation with God.

Lad; "Dear God, you're so awesome that a million years is like a minute to you."

God: "That's true son."

Lad: "Precious Lord, you're so great that a million dollars is like a cent to you."

God: "You're right again."

Lad: "My benevolent and merciful Creator since you're so powerful why don't you give me a million dollars?"

God: "Sure my child, that's a piece of cake. Just hold on for a minute." (1000000 yrs.)

MORAL: No one can outwit God in a life time so don't mess with the Father in Heaven.

92

Inter-racial Marriage Mix up

A rich Bahamian Chinese got married to a pure white woman from Eastern Heights. After a year of sublime, sweet marriage they were expecting their first child.

Upon delivery of the baby boy the Chinese husband went to visit the min Doctors' Hospital. Before entering the maternity ward, the nurse in attendance congratulated him and told him to come up with a name for the bundle of joyful surprise.

When Mr. Wong saw the baby boy in very dark complexion he declared loudly, "Sum ting Wong!" The nurse applauded and said, "That's a beautiful name."

MORAL: Loyalty in marriage goes beyond ethnic or racial boundaries.

93

Condoms Confusion and Carelessness

A Chinese entrepreneur, who became a naturalized Bahamian, visited his doctor to find ways to stop having more children.

"Doc, my wife and I already have six children and we don't want anymore."

To which the doctor added, "But you still want to enjoy sex, eh?" The Chinese beamed a bright smile and nodded.

"Well, here's a pack of condoms. Use one every time you're going to have sex with your wife." Within a few months the wife got pregnant despite the use of condoms.

He returned to the doctor and complained that his wife got pregnant in spite of the use of condoms.

The doctor asked him to describe how he went about using the condoms.

"Every time I put one on it was too long so I use a pair of scissors to cut off the extra piece hanging infront."

MORAL: One size fit all is a no-brainer.

The Poverty of Psychiatry

A housewife from Bimini visited a psychiatrist in Nassau and complained of hearing voices and movements under her bed at nights.

Doc.: "Who's making the noises and movements?" Housewife: "I don't know. I look under the bed and see no one, it's scary indeed."

The doctor did a one-hour session with her sitting on the couch recounting her experiences. At the end of the session, she was billed$180. The doctor told her to come back ever week for the next two months to have a complete cure.

Not seeing or hearing from the patient for two weeks the psychiatrist called her up to find out why she was not continuing her treatment.

Not wanting to continue paying such high bills the housewife said: "My husband found a solution. He sawed off the four legs of the bed."

MORAL: Common sense, rather than hefty professional consultation, can solve many maladies.

Psychological Prowess

Mr. Johnson from Over-the Hill suffered a heart attack and was admitted at PMH for treatment. The day before admission he had bought a lottery ticket. His wife, to her surprise, discovered that he won the jackpot of millions.

Not knowing how to break the good news to her husband who's nursing a heart condition she hired the professional help of a leading psychiatrist to deliver the breaking news. He visited Mr. Johnson in hospital and after exchanging pleasantries he calmly said, "Mr. Johnson if I told you that you won the jackpot of millions of dollars what would you do?"

"I would give you half of it." The good doctor dropped dead.

MORAL:

a) In your deathbed you can give away anything.

b) The ability to prepare for surprises and the unexpected opens the gateway to longevity.

Chicken Consolation

Mrs. Green lives in Farmers' Cay all by herself in her modest abode. Her four children went to school in Nassau and after graduation they took up jobs and are now living in town. Back home mother is growing old, lonely and downcast so they each decide to send her a pet to keep her company. One gives her a goldfish; one sends a puppy; the third one donates a cat and the youngest, Larry, gives her a peacock.

After a few weeks Larry calls to find out about her pets. Mama said, "Too much work to look after the fish, the cat keeps nannying on the bed, the dog always barking loudly. But thank you Larry the peacock was delicious."

MORAL: People are happy with what please the palates.

The Spelling Genius

In Cabbage Hill, Crooked Island a teacher was doing Spelling with her grade 1.

A five-year-old was asked to spell... INK. . . He started with Ethen flustered and failed. The teacher spanked him and the rest of the class laughed out loudly.

Pretending to be brave the boy put on a show and said loudly "I en k" (Meaning I don't care) The teacher turned around to face him and said, "You finally got it right."

MORAL: Frustration and embarrassment can produce effective and salutary solutions.

Empty Ex-ray

Johnny was carelessly riding his bicycle in Mangrove Cay when he crashed headlong into a car. He was flown out to Nassau for medical attention. After treatment and x-rays he was discharged. Upon returning home his mother asked him about his PMH experiences.

Johnny: "They X-rayed my head."

Mother: "And what did they find?"

Johnny: "Nothing."

His sister jeered, "I thought so." Empty head.

MORAL: Exercise caution when you reveal personal particulars.

Miraculous Misinterpretation

A 70-year-old man from Elizabeth Estate, New Providence felt down and depressed so he visited his doctor for help. The good doctor examined him thoroughly and finally put down his stethoscope and said, "Heart Murmur. Be careful."

A week later the doctor encountered the man walking along Cable Beach strip with a young, sexy girl hand in hand. He was so excited, walking on cloud nine to see his doctor.

Doctor: "Man you look so happy and hilarious. What's the secret?" 70-year-old: "Doc I took your advice and got me a hot mamma."

Doctor: "I didn't say that. I said H-E-A-R-T M-U-R-M-U-R. Be careful."

MORAL: Optimistic and cheerful patients can improvise positive prescription to remedy their ailment.

The Plurality of Politicians

A prosperous, proud and popular politician from Coral Harbor, NP took his spouse to see the family doctor when she complained about a sudden, sharp pain in her stomach.

Upon examination it was found out that she had a severe case of appendicitis. She underwent an emergency operation and survived. One year later the politician called upon the same Physician and said, 58 "Doc my gal is complaining about a sharp pain in her tummy. I think it'sher appendix."

Doctor looked him squarely in the face and responded, "Are you kidding me. One woman cannot have two appendices. Your wife had her appendix removed last year."

The politician sheepishly shored up something from his sleeve, "But a man can have two women, eh."

MORAL: Medical experts know little or nothing outside their field of expertise.

Sex for Text

In these digital days people will do almost anything to get in to the glamorous game of social media drama.

Recently a 16-year-old girl returned home in Yellow Elder and excitedly greeted her strict, single parent mother and boasted, "Guess what mummy.

I got a brand-new cell phone that I can call and text with." The mother showed interest and concern, "How did you get it?" Girl replied, "I traded sex for text with a man up the road."

Exasperated the mother boldly bawled out, "What!! Young lady you go right back and return that damn phone and take back your sex."

MORAL: That's a double whammer. Technology dazzles, delights, degrades and then destroys.

Population Explosion

In the olden days in Inagua people were having babies like crazy. One woman got 8 children through her first marriage. A year later when her husband died, she remarried and gave birth to 8 more children before the second husband died. Soon after that she died too.

At the funeral the pastor whilst preaching looked up to heaven and said, "Thank God they are together finally." The sister of the deceased mildly interrupted, Father what do you mean they are together. Do refer to her being together with her first or second husband?"

The gracious Father replied righteously, "No my dear. I mean her legs."

MORAL:

a) Some preachers go down to earth to make their messages simple and easily understood.

b) The invention of contraceptives, be it condom or the pill, has averted a population explosion in the country.

The Birth of Babies

A six year the old, eldest of four children, was driven by curiosity to ask her mother. "Where do babies come from?" The mother, not wanting to share the blessings and beauty of biology, soberly responded, "Babies come from planes."

When the fifth baby was due and the mother lapsed into labor the husband rushed to take her to the hospital. Six-year-old sharply interrupted, "Where are you taking mom?"

"To the hospital to get her baby." replied dad.

"No! You must take her to the airport."

"Why?" enquired the father.

"Her babies come from planes."

MORAL:

a) Deliberately hiding the truth can open the window to original creativity and brilliance.

b) When honesty and reality is suppressed, lively imagination goes in gear.

Sweet Sensation of Pronunciation

In a senior high school in Nassau a teacher asked the class a fundamental question: What is sex?

A smart Alec answered: Sex is a sinful 'Temptation' with the deep 'Sensation' and a 'Passion' where a male uses his 'Erection' for 'Penetration' into a female 'Destination' to have 'Satisfaction' and to increase the 'Population' for the next 'Generation' to continue God's 'Creation'. Teacher, do you understand my 'Explanation' or do you want a 'Demonstration'?

The female teacher fainted.

MORAL: Sex 'Education' can shore up incredible 'Information' from student 'Population' in this modern 'Generation' to shock you beyond 'Expectation' so use 'Caution' when you ask the next 'Question'.

Brotherly Brew

In a posh, peace and plenty pub in Georgetown Exuma a patron entered and ordered two tall glasses of whisky and slowly savored sips from both glasses one after the other until empty. He did that on a routine basis every evening. The curious bartender inquired "Why do you regularly drink two glasses of whisky?"

"I have a dear brother who has gone to live in Nassau. Whilst he was here, we both enjoyed drinks together. Now he is gone I drink two glasses for both of us. One for him and one for me." replied the faithful customer.

After a few months he came in and as soon as the bartender saw him, he started to pour drinks in two glasses. The patron told him to make that one glass to which the bartender remarked, "What happen? Something wrong with your brother?"

"No. Nothing is wrong with my brother. He is well and doing fine." answered the guy.

"Then why are you having one glass today?" quizzed the bartender.

"I quit drinking," said the happy drinker as he polished the content of comfort.

MORAL: Never satisfy or save yourself by trying to please family or friend

Worshiping wealth

A gentleman from Freeport Grand Bahama grew up to be a faithful Christian who attended church regularly.

Then suddenly he stopped going to church. One day the priest of his church met him and asked why he was not attending church anymore. He said, "Father, to be brutally frank I have found a new God which is money…wealth to worship…and I am very happy now."

"After several years he returned to church, dejected and depressed. As soon as the priest saw him, he welcomed him with open, gracious arms. Then he asked, "What brought you back to church?"

"Father I am dead broke." he coyly responded.

MORAL: Money and material wealth are transient and fleeting but your Creator who gave your life and the world is permanent and everlasting. Be holy and steadfast.

The Divine Duel

At a religious retreat in Cat Island priests from all over the Bahamas gathered to re-calibrate, rejuvenate and re-energized after long spell of church duties in various islands. During coffee breaks they listened to snippets of humorous highlights from laymen. One man rose to tell a joke.

"There was a time when Jesus, Moses and a Third Person played golf. Moses took the first shot and hit the ball within the reach of the green patch. Jesus told Moses that was an excellent shot. When Jesus struck the ball, it went and landed on a dry spot in the middle of a pond. Jesus walked on water and made a second swipe which took the ball inches from the hole in the middle of the green. And Moses said "good shot Jesus "When the Third player hit the ball it dropped in the middle of the pond and a huge fish caught it in its mouth and powerfully spat it out to land near the hole and a squirrel from nowhere appeared and nudge edit into the winning hole. And Jesus said "Great shot Dad"

MORAL: Whatever you do don't mess with God because you will never win no matter how powerful or mighty you are.

The Mailboat Matter

During a long mailboat ride from Ragged Island to Potters Cay dock in Nassau a disheveled half-drunk guy sat next to a reverend Father reading a newspaper. His demeanor and smell upset the priest who did not complain nor moved away. Then the boozy guy leaned over and asked "Father what is arthritis" Disgusted by his bad-breadth the priest sharply answered. "People who are sinful and evil, tell lies, cheat, abuse alcohol and drugs, and sexually molest minors get arthritis." After sailing for a few minutes, the priest felt bad to give such a crude answer and tried to mend matters. He said to the guy who was still reading his newspaper, "I didn't mean to give such a stern answer but why did you ask me that question? "The guy dropped the papers and said "The news say that the Pope has arthritis".

MORAL: Don't judge a book by its cover. Shabby or poor appearances never tell the true story. A little polishing can clear away the outer rust of gold and diamond.

109

The Wonders of Wine

After a fantastic tour of the beautiful fields of Flamingoes in Inagua in deep South Bahamas a young couple settled down in their suite having red wine. After a few drinks the wife remarked "I love you so very much my darling. I don't know what I can do without you."

A bit surprise and pleased the husband asked, "Is that you talking or the wine? "The wife confidently responded, "Yes my dear that' s me…. talking to my wine."

MORAL: Some expressions of love are full of empty surprises. Watch your words winos.

110

Allowance for the Aged

An elderly bald gentleman went to the Social Welfare Office in Nassau to apply for old age benefits. The seasoned female interviewer asked him for an ID or drivers' license.

Upon checking his pockets, he realized that he had forgotten his wallet home he told her that he didn't have it on his possession. The woman asked him to open his shirt.

When he obliged sheepishly the woman had a good look and saw the white silvery hair on his chest.

Satisfied she approved his application. As soon as he got home, he boasted to his wife.

"Guess what. I forgot my ID home and the woman just stared at my chest and approved my old age benefit. Can you believe it?"

Not too amused the wife said, "You should have dropped your pants to get disability allowance."

MORAL: Most people judge you by your outward appearance and attributes. Gray hair puts power on passports.

Cognitive Concur

In Eleuthera an old couple in their eighties have been experiencing problems remembering things so they visited their doctor for help. After recounting many instances of forgetfulness and unfortunate results the doctor said,

"Always write down things on a piece of paper. Things you have to do, where you have to go, names and dates and the like."

One day the wife asked the husband to go downstairs and make her breakfast of bacon and eggs. She directed that he writes it down to which the old guy said, Piece of cake. I will remember bacon and eggs." She added, 'And please get me French toast with garlic butter." Husband reassured her.

"Bacon and eggs with French toast with garlic butter coming up." After a long while he returned with a steaming bowl of chicken souse Bahamian style. The wife looked at it and smiled then complained

"You forgot the johnny bread."

MORAL: Dementia and Alzheimer are bad but they do have their share of good fortune. Remember the couple who forgot their flight that crashed.

112

Insulting In Laws

There was a couple living in Andros who always traded insults of their in-laws. Husband always complained about his mother-in-law. "I can't stand my mother-in-law. She is a bawling bitch." Wife typical response "My Father-in-law is a wicked old fart. I hate his bossy balls."

One day they were driving along the main road when they passed some cows grazing on the shoulders of the road. After a long silence the husband remarked, "Look at those skinny cows. I don't like their looks." To which the wife with a smirch responded, "Leave my in laws alone!"

MORAL: Wife always wins in lawful and in-lawful battles despite the husband winning the war. Don't treat in-laws as outlaws.

113

Sexual Slip

In Freeport Grand Bahama guy came home one evening and headed straight to his room where he saw his wife sleeping under cover. Not wanting to rudely disturb her he delicately lifts the sheet and went under and started to make love with his wife. After he had finished, he felt hungry suddenly and proceeded downstairs to get a sandwich. When he got into the kitchen he saw his wife there cooking. Surprised he asked, "How come you reach downstairs so quickly after making love?"

Taken back by his question she said she wasn't upstairs and told him that her mom visited and she complained of not feeling well so she told her to go upstairs and rest. Then it dawned upon her. "My God Henry you f-- ked my mom! "She rushed upstairs and addressed her mom in sharp tones. "Mom, you allowed Henry to make love to you. Why did you allow that.

Why didn't you say something to stop him? In a self-satisfied smirk she replied, "I haven't spoken to the bastard for over 10 years and I don't intend to start now."

MORAL: Undercover operation shores up rewarding surprises. Be careful when entering dark alleys.

The Plucky Push

A celebrity bigwig in Lyford Cay was boasting about his collection of alligators and sharks. He took a crowd to the pool where he kept his aquatic vultures.

People observed and took pictures. He challenged anyone to swim across the pool unharmed and offered a handsome reward for the brave person to do so. As soon as he finished offering the prize a guy jumped into the pool and hurriedly swam across the beast infested waters and in the nick of time he safely landed on the other side.

The celebrity agreed to deliver the prize but before he did so he asked the guy how come he mustered the courage to jump in the pool. In response the guy said, "I want to see the person who pushed me into the pool."

MORAL: When people are pushed, they can accomplish heroic feats. Surprises come when you least expect them. Be prepared and mindful.

Which Weed

In Staniel Cay on the Exuma chain of islands a policeman saw a fellow standing suspiciously on the pavement along a busy spot. He approached the fellow and asked him what he was doing there. He smelled ganja weed emanating from his person and he proceeded to interrogate him. He searched him and found few pounds of marawana in his jacket pocket."I arrest you for the possession of illegal drugs," and was about to take him into custody. The fellow in defense said, "Officer I keep trying to get rid of the darn stuff and it keeps coming back into my pocket."

The officer said, "I don't believe you. Do you want to show me how this happens? "The fellow asked him to follow him. He took him into a public washroom and emptied his pocket into the toilet and then flushed it down.

After some time, the officer searched his jacket and found no weed then he asked, "Where is the weed?"

"Which weed?"

MORAL: Smart criminals always find loopholes in the justice system. Stricter the government wiser the population.

The Drunk Drill

A proud father took his 18-year-old son to a bar for drinks. He offered his son a beer and he downed several whiskeys. He started to lecture his son on the habit of drinking. "Son you must not take too much drinks. That is not good. Moderation is the key. When you get drunk you can embarrass yourself.

At this point the son asked, "Dad how do you when you are drunk?

"The father squirted around the bar looking for a scenario to answer the question. "Son, you see those two men drinking at that corner "He pointed in that direction he mentioned. The son looked carefully and said, "Dad there is only one man there."

MORAL: It is not an easy task to be a role-model to the younger generation. Take fewer drinks to hold your head up.

Clocks of Confessions

Telling jokes at a party on the beautiful beach on Paradise Island one guy told a story where a man died and he ascended into heaven. He saw tons of clocks placed all over the place and asked St. Peter "Why are so many clocks displayed in heaven?"

St. Peter told him that they keep a record of lies people have told in their lifetime. Some clocks were going slow; some are stuck. The guy saw some that were running fairly fast and enquired. St. Peter told him that those represent salesmen and women. After some time, he asked to see the clocks of lawyers to which St. Peter said, "Those are so fast that we keep them in the office ceiling to cool us."

MORAL: Waste no time spreading lies. Someone is keeping score.

Diarrhoea Drug

In a school in Bennet' s Harbor Cat Island a teacher asked the class to name a medicine or drug and say its function. One girl said, "Aspirin. It is good for a headache.

"Very good Sarah, "said the teacher. Another student said, "Buckleys. It is good for cough and fever." The teacher approved and praise her answer. Little Johnny said, "Viagra. It is a cure for diarrhoea."

This surprised the teacher who asked Johnny to explain the function. Quite confidently little Johnny explained, "Last night I heard my mom tell my dad "Drink a Viagra it will harden your shit."

MORAL: Random relief can come from pharmaceutical confusion. Keep drugs away from children.

The Insistent Idiot

In a busy Supermarket in Cable Beach Nassau a customer and a salesman were seriously arguing over an issue concerning sales in the store. The argument grew loud and it aroused the attention of shoppers. Finally, the disgruntled customer barged out of the store. The manager who heard the furore, came up to the salesman and reprimanded him then said, "The customer is always right. See to it that all customers are treated right." the salesman tried to explain the crux of the matter but the manager stopped him in his track.

Before the manager moved away he asked the salesman, "What did the customer say?"

"He said that you are an idiot."

MORAL: Customers' preference has its side effects. The mouth you feed can turn back and bite you.

River of Rum

In a church in Duncan Town Ragged Island the pastor was preaching against the harm of drinking alcohol. "If I had all the beer in the world, I would throw it all in the river. If I had all the wine and whiskey in the world I would dump them in the river." He kept preaching about the problems caused by the use of alcohol. At the end of the sermon the congregation in one high, hallowed alto sang the hymn 'Let's gather by the river.'

MORAL: There is liquid Biblical support for drinks. Eat drink and be merry.

Embarrassing Evidence

In the High Court in Nassau Bahamas a case was being tried. After elderly took the oath and entered the box the defense council asked her "Mrs. Adams do you know me?"

"Of course, Mr. Ferguson. I know you since you were a child. You were naughty and nasty. When you grew up you told lots of lies and stole your neighbor's mangoes. You even beat up your wife and cussed out your mother in-law. Flabbergasted the lawyer faked a smile and pointed to the Prosecutor and asked if she knew him."

"Of course, I know Mr. Bradley since he was young. He grew up to be cunning and wicked. He gambles, drinks heavily, uses obscene language and has a lot of sweethearts one of them is your wife." rattled the woman.

At this point the judge summoned both the defense council and prosecutor to his desk and said in a husked voice, "If anyone of you asks her who I am I will send you to the electric chair."

MORAL: In no part of the world, you will find honest, decent and dignified professionals. Every character has a flaw or two. Learn to keep your closet clean.

Messy Message

A middle-aged couple in Fresh Creek Andros had just discovered the skill to text on their mobile phones. They practiced to exchange text messages to master the art. One weekend the wife went to Nassau.

While she was there, she sent few texts to him. "My darling husband if you are eating now send me a piece of the delicacy. If you are drinking post me a sip. And if you are sleeping send me the smell on the pillow."

The husband replied, "I am in the toilet, what do you want?"

MORAL: Novelty has its newly found pleasure but it comes with a hitch. Be cautious and thread safely.

Talented Tailors

In a barber shop in Clarence Town Long Island a few barbers on break were testifying on their inherent skills as tailors. One started with "I just have to look at a man and sew him a perfect suit." The second one boasted, "Just give me the name of the man and I will make a remarkable suit for him."

Not to be outdone the third tailor beaming with confidence bragged, "You just tell me the corner the man turns and I will produce a masterpiece suit for him."

MORAL: Exaggerated confidence and braggart can take one to higher heights. Empty boast is a balloon without air.

A Beer Butt

In the surgical department at Princess Margaret Hospital in Nassau a patient was taken into the doctor's room and prep by the attendant nurse for a colonoscopy examination. Whilst he was on the reclining bed he noticed a pair of gloves, a surgical syringe and a can of beer. Curious he wanted to know why the beer was placed there so when the doctor entered to do the examination he asked, "Doc why is a can of beer here?

"Exasperated" the doctor called in the nurse and scolded her, "I asked you to get a Butt light not a Bud light."

MORAL: Mistaken prescription can cause unforeseen problems.

The Immaculate Conception

A white lady from Eastern Height Nassau took her daughter to visit the doctor. The doctor asked what was the problem. The lady said, "My 17-

year-old daughter here is not feeling well. She complains of abdominal pains and getting morning sickness."

The good doctor took her into a private room for tests and examination. After a while he came out and told the lady that her daughter is four months pregnant. "What!", exclaimed the mother, "That is impossible. She hasn't met any man. She is a virgin being at home all the time." She turned to the daughter and asked if she ever had intercourse with anyone.

"No mom "replied the puzzled girl. The doctor briskly walked towards an opened window and stared outside for the longest while. After an anxious passage of time the lady addressed the family doctor. "What happens doc? Something wrong outside. What are you staring so hard at?"

The doctor took a deep breath and slowly said "I was looking for the bright Star in the east and the three wise men. I don't want to miss this episode that happened first long time ago in Bethlehem."

MORAL: Immaculate conception remains in the Bible; it doesn't happen in any modern miracle.

The Bartender Brew

A guy went into a bar in Arawk Cay and placed an order.

"P..ppleeasse g..iv. .e m..mee a b.beeer." The bartender noticed that the guy had a stuttering problem. The next day the same guy returned to the bar and stuttered an order for a beer. Being considerate and concerned the bartender offered an advice. "So sorry about your speech defect. At one time I too had the same problem but I have it solved when my wife gave me a blowjob three times. You must try that. Believe me it works."

The guy agreed and returned to the bar a couple days after and continued to stutter when he made his order. Worried the bartender asked, 'Didn't you try what I told you to?'

The guy with shameful satisfaction replied, "I tried exactly what you ordered but it hasn't worked. But you do have a nice house."

MORAL: Never be too loose or liberal with helpful advice, because it will come back to haunt you.

The Virtous Virgin

A very devout Christian woman in Acklins has been a virgin all her life. She never got married nor had any kind of relationship with any man. She vowed to be a virgin, and rightly so. As she grew older, she made an arrangement with an undertaker to etch selected words on her headstone;

HEREIN LIESAVIRGINWHOWAS NEVER MARRIEDAND GAVE HERLIFE TOCHRIST

The prepaid undertaker agreed so to do. When she died the undertaker asked his gravediggers to write the given words on her headstone. The lazy grave workers thought that it was too much work to etch in all those words so they engraved 'RETURNED UNOPENED'

MORAL: Be careful what you wish for.

128

Parody of Politics

One late evening a son in Fox Hill New Providence asked his dad. "Dad what is politics?" The astute father said, "Son that's a tricky question. Look at politics this way. As the father of this home, I make the money to get what we need. I am the Capitalist. Your mother is the Government, she runs things. You represent the People. Your younger brother represents the Future and the nanny is the Working Class."

That night they all went to sleep. During the middle of the night the son heard his younger brother crying so he went to see what happened. The brother was crying because he dumped in his diaper. The son went in his mom room to get help but noticed his mom fast asleep. So, he went to the nanny's room but the door was locked. He peered through the keyhole and to his amazement he saw his dad on top of the nanny making out. Disappointed he went back to sleep. The next morning at the breakfast table the dad enquired, "Son, have you figured out what is politics?"

"Yes dad. It' s like this. While the Capitalist is screwing the Working Class the Government is asleep and the People is ignored whilst the Future is in deep shit."

MORAL: Realities define the true meaning of politics. Poly tricks is the name of the game.

Capitalist Creation

In Elizabeth Estate in New Providence a youngster came home suddenly and found his mother making out with a sweet-man in bed. He quietly sneaked into the closet and watched on. Then he heard his father entering the house and announced his arrival. Quickly the wife hid her lover in the closet. Whilst inside the closet the boy said, "It is sure dark in here."

"Yes, it is," agreed the lover. The boy said, "I have a baseball to sell. You wanna buy it?"

"No" responded the lover. The boy threatened, "My dad is downstairs." OK. How much? whispered the sweet-man "$200".

The same scenario repeated itself the following week. And the boy sold his baseball gloves for $300.

One day the boy' s dad asked him to go outside to play 'Catch' The boy told his dad that he sold his ball and gloves." What! How much did you sell them for?

"$500 Dad"

"That's robbery. You cheated the buyer. I have to let you confess this Sunday at church." said his father.

In the confession cubicle the boy said, "It is dark in here, "Okay buster. How much for what you' re selling now?"

MORAL: Cheating gives rise to Capitalism. Sweet-hear thing is a costly pleasure

The Proud Professor

At the University of the Bahamas a slick student went to sit next to a professor in the canteen." Sir can I sit near you to have lunch?"

"No way! Pigs don't mix with pigeon. "Replied the Professor

"In that case I will flap my wings and fly away" replied the student making the teacher embarrassed. Not wanting to be dubbed a pig the Professor vowed to fail this saucy student. Among the tests he administered was an oral: "If you found two bags, one full with gold and the other filled with intelligence, and have to pick one which one would take?"

The student responded, "I would take the gold. Which one would you take?

With gleeful confidence the teacher said, "I would take the bag of intelligence."

"To which the student wisely remarked, "Naturally one would take the one that he lacks."

MORAL: Acting smart can reduce your opponent to zilch

The Cradle of Creation

One day a little girl in a town in Abaco asked her mom, "Mom where do humans come from?"

The thought for a while then said, "God created Adam and Eve and they produced children who later produced more children. That process went on for centuries to create a world of people." Later that day he met her dad in the garage and asked him the same question.

The dad scratched his head and said, "Long time ago we had apes and gorillas in Africa who evolved gradually to become humans."

Later she confronted her mom. "Mom, you said that God created human human family. And dad said that people came from apes and gorillas."

"Your dad' s family came from apes and gorillas," said mom seriously.

MORAL: The debate of Evolution and Creation has no end in the human race.

Parental Puzzle

In the heat of the night in a home in Nassau a boy came downstairs and shouted, "Mom I want to piss. I must piss now." The mother who was in the middle of a conversation with some friends felt embarrassed got up to take the little boy to the bathroom. Whilst there she cautioned him to be more polite next time he wanted to urinate.

"Next time you must say "Whisper"

Another time when mom was entertaining friends the boy came down to pee. This time he said, "Mom I want to Whisper. Whisper! "After taking him to relieve himself she complimented him on his improved behavior. One night he came down to pee but he found his dad there instead of mom. He called out, "Whisper. Whisper "His dad acknowledged his presence and said, "What you want to say? Come whisper in my ears."

MORAL: Parental guidance and upbringing must have clarity and unison to ensure harmonious development.

Sperm Surprise

An elderly man visited his doctor at Doctors' Hospital on Shirley Street in Nassau for his annual exam. Among the things the doctor ordered was to get a sperm count. So, he gave the man a sealed jar and asked him to bring back some of his sperms the next day.

The elderly man promptly returned the next day and presented an empty sealed jar. The doctor took one look and said, "What happened. This jar is empty."

The patient coyly answered, "I tried everything. My right hand, my left hand. I even asked my wife to help. She tried both hands and even put it between her legs. I also asked my neighbor to help. She tried her best and nothing happened." At this point the doctor interrupted, "You asked your neighbor?"

"Even her husband tried and couldn't open the jar. "

MORAL: Faulty medical equipment or prescription can result in unexpected surprises.

Healthy Habits

An old Caucasian gentleman and wife in their Eighties were asked by one of their club members about the secrets of living so healthy in their old age. The man said, "my wife and I quarrel every day. Whoever won the row gets to set a punishment. Being so smart, slick and cunning she always wins. So, she tells me to run 5 miles every day."

"The club members remarked, "Okay running everyday helps to make you healthy. But what does she do to be equally healthy?"

"She runs behind me to see that I complete the 5 miles," responded the white guy.

MORAL: Daily exercise with your wife or a companion is good for you.

The Motor Mistake

A white 85-year-old man took his white pregnant 18-year-old wife to the maternity ward in a private hospital in Freeport Grand Bahama to give birth to a baby. After a successful delivery the friendly nurse asked the old man how he managed to accomplish such a feat. To which he sheepishly replied,

"Oh blessed" Savior! I just keep oiling the old motor, "boasted" the man.

The following year he took the wife again to the same hospital to give birth. After she handed the new born to the old father the same nurse complimented him. Continuing to boast the man remarked, "Nurse" I keep oiling the motor, "The kind nurse firmly responded," This baby is black. You need to change the oil in your motor.

MORAL: Not all old motors run efficiently and effectively and faithfully.

Trendy Technology

A guy in Nassau complained to a friend that he had a terrible headache saying, "This headache doesn't want to go away. I must see a doctor."

"Don't waste money seeing a doctor. There is a computer in the Pharmacy a block away. Just apply some of your urine on a s lot and put in $5 to get immediate diagnosis and treatment." advised the friend. Knowing that high tech and AI can do anything he gave it a try. Applying the sample of his urine in a designated slot and putting in $5 he heard the computer come to life with sounds and lights. Finally, it produced a slip of paper which read; Migraine. Rest a lot; drink lots of liquid; don't stress yourself and drink Aspirin. Amazed by the advanced development of technology he decided to trick the computer. He took a sample of tap water, drops of his dog's urine and little urine from his teenage daughter and wife.

He even added some oil from his car. He applied the tricky sample to the computer and paid the $5. As usual the computer kicked into gear with different neon lights. Then it pushed out a strip of paper which read: Tap water is polluted; dog has worms; daughter is pregnant; wife has traces of sperms from three different men and your car needs a new oil filter. No wonder you have headache.

MORAL: Modern high technology is capable of fascinating and outsmarting mankind.

Pointless Pretence

A young man fresh from law school in the USA returned to set up his practice in Bay Street Nassau. On the first day upon opening his impressive office a man came through the passage way towards his office. As soon as the man entered the bright barrister took up his phone pretending to impress his client. He spoke into the receiver, "I am too busy to take that case which only pays $100000. If fees are duly increased, I will definitely condescend." While on the phone with his pretense, he waved to the man to take a seat. Resting the phone down, he politely greeted the would-be client with a big smile.

"Sorry about the call. How can I help you?" The man replied, "I came to hook up your phone."

MORAL: Pretense does not guarantee authenticity. Be truthful and humble when dealing with people.

Dear Dog

A young girl in Spanish Wells Eleuthera wanted to take their dog out for a walk so she asked her mom. "Mom, can I take Lily out for a stroll?"

"No. The dog is in heat so you cannot take her anywhere," answered the mom. Not giving up she approached his dad who was busy in the garage.

"Dad, I want to take the dog out but mom says she is in heat and I must not take Lily out," said the girl. Not wanting to disappoint the poor child he poured some gasolene on the dog's behind and allowed the girl her wish.

After some time, the girl returned without the dog and the dad asked what happened. The girl said, "Half way down the road the gas ran out and another dog is towing Lily home."

MORAL: Pleasing children is a risky business.

Sweet Sexual Sacrifice

A poor old man in Nassau was in his deathbed waiting on his appointed hour to kick the bucket. He waived to his wife to come sit beside him. Settling down he said in a weak voice, "My darling tells me. During our marriage life did you cheat on me with other men?"

Summoning courage she admitted, "Yes. One time we couldn't pay our mortgage and I settled that with the banker. Another time we needed money to make our car payment. That I solved with the salesman. And remember the time you needed 12 votes to be the President of your golf club. That was when I got you the winning votes."

MORAL: Some dedicated wives can go to any lengths to please their husbands. Sweet sensual sacrifice secures success

The Danger of a Decent Deal

A Landlord in Nassau was out one night for fun. He managed to get a call girl for the night having pleasures of the flesh for an agreed sum of $500. When he was about to leave, he realized that he didn't have his wallet so he promised the wench to send her a cheque. In due course he sent a cheque for $250 with the following considerations.

A. You claimed that you were pretty, cozy and tight but you turned out to be slack, loose and overused.

B. Your rented apartment had no heat and rhythm

C. Your apartment was too large

Because of these reasons I am paying you half price.

The lady of the night returned the cheque with the following response.

A. What do you expect from a beautiful apartment that is attractive to countless renters.

B. My apartment always has heat and rhythm but you did not know how to turn it on.

C. My apartment is the ideal size but you had not the furniture to fit in it.

If you don't send the full $500, I will let your landlady know everything. In the very next mail, she received her full payment.

MORAL: In every business deal know the terms of agreement and engagement before execution. Looks and promises are deceptive and can have negative consequences.

Professional Pranks

A doctor in Freeport Grand Bahama decided to make quick bucks by not very professional means. He posted a big sign in front his office which reads: -

For $20 I CAN CURE ANY SICKNESS. IF I FAIL, I PAY $100.

A lawyer saw the sign and decided to give it a shot. He entered the doctor's office and complained that he lost his sense of taste and made his payment. Immediately the doctor ordered his assistant to bring Formula 25 and he instructed the patient to drink it.

This he did obediently and spat it out in disgust "Shit this is gasolene!"

"Okay you have your sense of taste restored," claimed the good doctor.

The next visit the lawyer decided to try his luck again. "Doctor, I have lost my memory. I don't remember things anymore."

The dear doctor collected his $20 and called on his assistant to bring Formula 25 to which the lawyer reacted, "Don' t brings that stuff that' s gasolene."

"Well Sir your memory is back to normal, "pronounced the fair doctor.

Not satisfied and wanting to redeem his lost he went back to the doctor a third time. "Doc I can't see. I have lost my sight."

The good doctor confessed that he could not remedy that so he handed the lawyer a one-dollar bill. "Common Doc, you can't fool me. This is not $100 you promised."

"Well, I am glad that your sight is fully restored."

MORAL: Not all professionals are fully professional. Some profess practices prudently to prime profits primarily.

The Jewish Jingle

While conducting a Literature lesson a teacher asked her students few questions and promised that each correct answer would be rewarded with the rest of the day off.

Who said: "Ask not what your country can do for you; ask what you can do for your country."

A Jewish girl quickly said: "John Kennedy." Johnny didn't have the chance to give his answer and got angry.

Teacher told the girl to leave for her free time off. She politely refused saying that she preferred to stay on and learn. "Who said: Bethe change you want to see in the world." A Jewish boy shouted, "Mahatma Gandhi" Johnny was exasperated that he couldn't give the correct answer in time.

The boy followed the girl decision to remain in class.

As the teacher turned to write something on the board Johnny exclaimed "These f... ... Jews must be eliminated. "Suddenly the teacher turned to face the class," who said that?

"Johnny answered," Adolph Hitler first said that.

"The teacher responded," Johnny you can go for the week. Guess what! Don't ever come back.

MORAL: Impatience is a powerful force that could evoke great mischief. Control and discipline are required to temper it. Jewish mentality and attitude make them the riches people on earth.

The Betting Beauty

A very beautiful lady went to bank some money. She approached the teller and told her that she had a large sum of money to deposit in her savings. The teller tried to help but the woman demanded to see the bank manager. Reluctantly she allowed her to come in to the manager's office.

Manager said, 'What can I do to help you maam? 'The elderly woman emptied a bag full of money in the tune of 250000 dollars. The manager was astonished and asked, "Where do you get such large sum of money?" The woman replied that she did lots of betting. The manager couldn't believe her.

The lady said, "I can show you. I bet you 50000 dollars that your testicles are square."

"No way! Your bet is on." "Tomorrow I will bring my lawyer to witness the bet," said the female.

The next morning the manager bathed and thoroughly checked out his round testicles to confirm their natural god given shapes. Confidently he went tohis office to cash in on his big bet.

Promptly at 9 am the woman returned with her lawyer. In the secluded office the lady requested that the manager dropped his pants to reveal his grapes. Shyly he agreed and lowered his trousers to fully expose his seminal organs.

The woman held both in her hands and fingered them around while the lawyer witnessed the sexy show. Then the lawyer took out his cheque book and wrote the lady a cheque for 100000 dollars. The manager couldn't understand what was going on so he enquired.

The lucky lady told him: "I bet the lawyer that I could play with the bank manager's balls, which I happily did. And they are firmly round and warm. Thank you very much. Here is your 50000 dollars."

MORAL: Look out for the catch in every bet. The House always wins in the long run.

Blessed Blaspheme

A religious knowledge teacher asked: "Where can you find Jesus Christ?" One girl said, "In your heart". The teacher approved her response.

Another girl said, "Jesus is found in all churches where Christian's worship."

The teacher supported all the positive answers with favorable comments.

Little Johnny said: "Jesus is found in the bathroom." The teacher along with some students went aghast. Then little Johnny explained: "This morning when my dad went to the bathroom and tried the door handle, he blurted out: Jesus Christ! you are still in there!!"

MORAL: Try to avoid blasphemous expressions by not sleeping on the toilet. Never use the name

Paint My Porch

A rich businessman in Nassau wanted to have his front porch painted so he engaged a painter to do the job. He gave the painter detailed instructions to follow. "Paint the porch from bow to stern fully in green. I will pay you well for a good job done

"The painter finished the job under 30 minutes and then reported to the boss in his mansion. "Sir I am finished painting"

"What! So quickly. That lengthy porch should have taken a full day to complete."

"It didn't take long to paint the Porche. I gave her two coats of paint. I can do the Ferrari for the same price."

The businessman was shocked to see his sports car daubed in regular paint.

MORAL: Specific instructions for any job must be followed by supervision to avoid mistakes. A play on words can create surprises wonderful or woeful.

146

Remorseless Rebound

A lady and her 6 years old daughter were travelling in a taxi around Freeport, Grand Bahama in the night.

As they passed along a popular street, they saw a number scantily dressed women standing at strategic spots. The daughter asked, "Mommy who are those women standing along the street?"

"Honey they are women waiting for their husbands to pick them up."

The cab driver overheard the conversation and chipped in, "Mam why don't you tell your daughter the truth that those women are prostitutes waiting for business?"

Then the daughter asked, "Mom do those women have children?" "Of course. That's how we get cab drivers."

MORAL: There is much wisdom in silence. Unnecessary interference in peoples' conversations can cause much embarrassment. The price of truth always hurts.

Rewarding the Reliable

A faithful longtime worker in a large corporation in downtown Nassau asked his boss for a raise. "Boss I have been working with your company for 20 years without any promotion or raise in salary. Other companies are ready and willing to take me on for good cash."

The boss didn't want to lose such a reliable worker so he gave the man an instant raise of pay with a year' s back pay. Then he enquired "Which are the companies that are willing to take you on?"

Smiling the worker replied, "The Electricity company", the Water company, the Telecommunication company, the Mortgage company. Bills and more bills.

MORAL: Smart approaches and brave risks can bring rewards.

Heavenly Havoc

A young couple died and went to Heaven. After being processed by St. Peter they asked if they could get married in Heaven. St. Peter promised to check and walked off. A long time passed and the couple did not hear anything from St. Peter. When he finally showed up, he said "Yes you could get married here."

The couple was pleased to hear this. Upon second thought they asked if things didn't work out if they could get a divorce.

Exasperated St. Peter said, "It took me three months to find a priest up here to do the marriage. Do you have any idea how long it will take to find a lawyer up here? "

MORAL: Entry into Heaven is difficult for men in robes. If you have to marry do so when you are alive

149

Drunken Disaster

In Carol Harbour in New Providence a woman was having a great time with her sweetheart in bed when they heard her husband opening the door to get in his house. The sweet man panicked and asked her what to do. "Must I jump out the window or hide under the bed?" "No. Just remain in bed and lay quietly. He always comes in drunk and wouldn't know a thing." said the woman confidently. The husband struggled up the stairs and slipped in bed under the cover next to his wife.

Before he dozed off, he looked down at the foot of the bed and saw six legs. Startled he enquired, "How come I see six feet in bed?

"The wife firmly replied," You see double when you are drunk. Go check it out.

There are four. "He got out of bed and examincd the feet in bed." "One, two, three, four. You are right honey, I'm sorry." He returned to bed and promptly fell asleep and the sweet man left.

MORAL: In sexual infidelity women are far smarter than men. Men 83 concentrate on their exploit and not on being exploited and women are the reverse. Being drunk limits one capacity to observethe realities in life. Learn to bring balance between bottle and beauty.

Handsome, Hardworking, Healthy and Hilarious Husbands

There is a freak store in Nassau that sells husbands. Inquisitive and curious women sneak in to discover the wonders of having a perfect husband. Rules are posted in front: -.

1. There are 4 levels to go up to see varying qualities of husbands, once you keep going up you cannot descend.

2. You can buy at any level and cash out

3. There is a surprise at the top level.

One enterprising woman started the climb. On the first-floor she read; "Husbands here are Handsome and Hardworking and they cost $ 500".

She wanted to see what' s upstairs so she climbed on. Second floor read: 'Husbands here are Handsome, Hardworking and Healthy' for $ 600. Encouraged she decided to venture upwards. Third floor read:

"Husbands here are Handsome, Hardworking, Healthy and Hilarious for $ 700."

Excited she made up her mind to go up and see the Surprise of a Perfect husband. Fourth floor read: "There are No husbands for sale at this level. Pay $1000 before you can exit"

MORAL: Women are very hard to please. There is nothing like a perfect husband. Learn to be content with the quality of current husband. Accepting and appreciating what you have goes a long way to protect and preserve the pleasure, peace and longevity of marriage. Qualities of people come in varying proportions.

POEMS

BAHAMIAN SUNRISE

What a spectacle and a surprise!
To warmly welcome a Bahamian sunrise,
Gradually emerging from the eastern horizon,
Ushering in light and energy there on,

Dispelling the darkness of the passing night,
Starting a new day, bold and bright.
Observe the initial crimson color,
Providing a background of grandeur.

Darkness slowly, smoothly, reluctantly
Disappearing reluctantly As the sun inches up in intensity
And the first arc of glowing light
Pushes its way up a watery or cloudy sight.

Glistening, growing in works of wonder
With her rising resonance growing wider,
Detect the dancing of shining shades,
As the remnant of the night finally fades,

See the rays of the rising sun,
Penetrate clouds hanging around,
Like a mammoth searchlight,
Searching for the thief in the night.

Read the message of the rising sun.
Greeting with glee, one shouldn't shun.
Offering fulsome freshness, opening the way,
Introducing one to the blessings of a new day.

Seek after the secret of the rising sun,
Telling all that a new life has begun.
Where there's light, there's a way.
To all the opportunities it has in sway,

Its brightness at the beginning of the day
Has sealed the fate and factors of yesterday.
Dutifully drawing one's attention to the now
To make the best of the day somehow.

Watch passing clouds fidgeting in fun,
as they salute the sacred sun.
Shivering stars shed their light and disappear.
As the sunlight grows in gear and glare,

With a brilliant burst of proud power,
The sun slowly skirts the sky with pleasure.
Eagerly engaged in its daily duty towards sunset,
without any flaw, rupture, or regret.

Never allow the sunrise to greet you in bed.
Be up and about with an alert, mindful head.
Be empowered by its energy to revel in its radiance,
In a wonderfully, enriching and enjoying a new day's experience.

A BAHAMIAN SUNSET

No natural beauty being presented yet,
To rival, surpass a Bahamian sunset,
A signature spectacle to savor in style,
Witnessing the sun setting in the watery wild.

Slowly, silently coming down
Against a bewitching, brilliant background
Magically moving with cheerful charm
Into the crimson curtain's open, awesome arms.

This breath-taking, passing panorama
Nothing short of a perfect, pleasant
Drama, bound to catch and capture
The hearts and admiration of every onlooker.

The sun seems to sink with reluctant willingness
into the hungry horizon of darkness
As it inches into the waving water
In a crescendo of colors and splendor.

Celebrating a ceremony of momentary magic
of the evening, endearing and ecstatic,
She seductively skirts the skyline
With a kiss to the briny brilliance, sweet and sublime.

In a flash of fleeting romance,
On a concave of lights in a divine dance,
Settling safely into the heavenly horizon,
Signifying submission in graceful abandon.

At the end of another day,
In her own special, wonderful way,
As she slides halfway under,
Beauty and brilliance stand still together.

One praises and laments the masterpiece moment
Of a passing, pleasant, priceless pageant,
Perfect time for a picturesque photo,
Captivating this imposing, impressive show.

Sinking deeper into a final resting place,
She maintains poise and grandeur with grace,
And, with a sparkling smile and a sweet sigh,
She goes under with a glistening goodbye.

Her final flashing of a brief, gorgeous green Light,
betokening the beginning of a new night,
Swallowed by the suction of the sea.
She leaves a lingering light in its locality.

Following Nature's immutable law in due diligence,
she's gone, resting in reverence
To the clever Creator and divine Designer
Of such an incomparable, unique extravaganza.

Let your sunset be a superlative spectacle,
A superb sensation ending in the making of a miracle,
of an exotic, exhilarating experience,
concluding your day with restful radiance.

BAHAMIAN BEACHES

Behold the beautiful Bahamian beaches,
Easily within everyone's reaches.
Layered, laden with white sand,
Etched at the edges of the mainland,

Stretching silently for many miles,
Waking wonders and smiles.
Merrily made by the hands of the Creator,
And not the genius of a contractor,

Been sitting silently, pure, prime, and premium
In their natural setting for many a millennium,
Only to be disturbed by the Lucayans,
The first Bahamian inhabitants.

The beach's a pretty place to play,
Each and every sunny day.
Great for outdoor games,
With no roads or lanes.

Suitable sites for parties and Picnics.
Full of fun and frolics.
Smell the smoke with a thrill
Coming from cooked meat on a grill.

Wend your way along the stretch of sand,
Walking with your lover hand in hand,

Inhaling the refreshing breeze,
As long as you please.

Let feet fall flat, Unrestrained,
On the gritty, Golden grains,
With toes digging deep
And feeling the sand rise from its sleep.

Smoothly, softly scrubbing the skin,
Giving a sweet Sensation within,
A bonus curative cleanser,
And a therapeutic texture.

Watch the water washing the strand,
Busily bathing each grain of sand,
Making them as white as snow,
With a wondrous, gleaming glow.

The clear, constant water works in waves,
As it laps or lashes in friendly or furious ways,
Deftling declaring that sand and Water
In wedlock stick and stay together.

You cannot have one without the other,
Since they are never put asunder.
A signature show of Mother
Nature, Designing a deed for our pleasure.

As you walk along the sandy spells,
Search for the slight specs of sea Shells,
Remains, relics from sea creatures,
Lazily laid there by incoming waters.

Notice how beach-goers dress sparingly,
Covered in shorts or a bikini.
Dipping, diving, or swimming,
Jetsking, surfing, and snorkeling,

Or simply lying on the soft sand.
Sun-bathing for a trendy natural tan,
A glorious gift with a natural brand
From the land of sun, sea, and sand.

The beach greets folks in the morning
As they come for brisk walking or jogging,
Being a bright, favorite facility,
Making them physically fit and healthy.

The beach's a retreat to relax readily.
Rewinding, recharging mind and body.
It opens up avenues and ambience
For yoga, meditation, and prayerful reverence.

A perfect place providing Opportunity
to express Childlike creativity,
Building sandy structures, stately standing,
Till the next wave comes crashing and tumbling.

The briny liquid lapping on the sand,
Crystal clear in the cup of your hand,
Its turquoise appearance graduating to a royal blue,
Stretching wide and deep into the ocean view.

Most hotels rise robustly near a beach,
Providing guests with an easy, comfortable reach
And enhancing the natural beauty of their surroundings
With an awesome, full, and fascinating

Bahamian beach, which is an A+ attraction
For visitors on vacation.
Packed with the power to please,
Like nectar to birds and bees,

With its magic and miracle,
The beach is indeed a superb spectacle,
A special treat to enjoy
By man, woman, girl, and boy.

From land, sea, or above,
It's a splendid sight everyone will love.
It's God's gift of glory,
Helping to swell our economy,

Providing a living and profit
For all involved in it.
So, keeping it clean is a must
By each and everyone of us.

THE BAHAMIAN PEOPLE

The small but proud Bahamian
Population is made up of people from many nations.
Some are of European descent,
Majority stemmed from the African continent.

Being descendants of people from many lands,
Proud products of Lucayans, Europeans, and Africans,
Coming together, commingling, and reproducing,
Spawning a society slowly growing.

Pure, full-blooded Lucayan inhabitants
Disappeared, blended in the blood of descendants,
With DNA and physical features
Imprinted in countless colored characters.

Resulting in sapodilla brown
Traces on the skin of lovely, round
Faces, sporting a kinky hair trait,
Dark, coarse, longish but not straight.

African blood is freely mixed with other Races.
The aftermath of slavery down ages.
By the promiscuity perpetrated by the powerful,
Resulting in all ethnic shades and potential.

The colonial ruling white minority
Tried hard to maintain racial integrity.

Unable to prevent their blood spilling into the veins
Of other races in the social train.

The concourse of color and Characteristics
grows gracefully in genders and genetics,
Manifesting a medley of a unique population
with little or no racial conflict or contention.

Some were cradled in the Caribbean,
With a large group of Haitians,
Surviving in the social Melting pot,
sharing a common lot.

A peaceful and friendly combination.
Inspite of different skin complexion,
Pledged to progress forever,
Going upward, onward together.

Though scattered all over the Archipelago,
They have and hold a common motto,
Set in separate settlements,
Being led by a democratic government.

Basically, following a Christian religion,
With its multiple denominations
Flocking in faithful fellowship,
Sailing the stream in a solemn ship.

Living in the lap of luxury or humble homes,
With family and friends of their own,
Busy with bustling brands of business,
or pursuits they cannot resist.

Earning a living in a tourist destination,
With varying degrees of reward and consolation,
Always provides playtime for pleasure,
On weekends and during leisure hours.

Happily, engaged in sports, games, or parties,
Or on vacation with friends and families,
With open arms, they greet strangers
Without asking for favors.

Blessed with the gift, grace of giving,
And the art, knack of socializing,
Despite occasional friction and tragedy,
A price paid by any society.
Which, like any dark cloudy day,
Will soon pass and go away.

LESS IS MORE

Current trends and prevailing philosophy
Entail and engages more effort and energy
To keep up with the crowd and the jury
In the fray of a futile fit of fury

Success means more hard work and sacrifices
More pressure, push and painful price
Less time for the pursuit of peace, pause and pleasure
Deprived of the significant stuff of life that really matter

The establishment and enhancement of status
Demands accumulation of more things to possess
More wealth, more vehicles, more personal property
Requiring more responsibility, safety and security

Having less and needing less of everything
Provides psychological strength and spring
To freely jump from limb to limb
To soar, swagger, sail or swim

Having less material weight to carry
Physically lighten mind and body
Material possessions represent additional weight
Making it difficult to walk steady and straight

Having more increases the fear of loss
Of the things attained at a high cost

Having less means nothing or little to lose
Conferring copious compass and confidence to cruise

Augmented attachment to accumulated assets
Consumes time, resources and energy on the offset
Freezing freedom and lessened leisure to explore
The beauty and blessings of life galore

The act of achieving more and more
Carries the onus of obligations to save and secure
Thus, delivering a dent to peace of mind
And activating anxiety and stress of all kind

Less clinging on to material things
Releases more energy, time for freelancing
And more leverage and latitude to live life
More fully, focused, frugally, with less stress and strife

Less is more in many wonderful ways
Greater freedom, peace, tranquility and longer days
Reduced cost, confusion, complexity and crisis
Less sanctifies the scope for comfort and happiness

THINGS TO DO IN THE BAHAMAS

- Tours and Sightseeing
- Boat Rides (Speedboat, Sailing)
- Swimming with the Pigs
- Jet Ski Adventure
- Reef Snorkeling / Deep Sea Diving
- Sunset Dinner Cruise
- Island Hopping by Sea or Air
- Rum and Wine Tasting
- Parasailing
- Glass Bottom Boat Tours
- Sports Fishing
- Nassau Rum, Reggae and Rhythms
- Private Yacht Party Charter
- Interactive Pirate Ship Cruise
- Junkanoo Fun and Party
- Casino
- Horseback Riding
- Disco
- Beach Barbeques
- Shopping
- Golfing and Ball Games

www.ingramcontent.com/pod-product-compliance
Lightning Source LLC
Chambersburg PA
CBHW050002040726
47599CB00014B/1180